KADE
SHADOWRIDGE GUARDIANS MC

KATE OLIVER

This book is a work of fiction. Names, characters, organizations, places, events, and incidents are either a product of the author's imagination or are used fictitiously. Any resemblance to actual persons, living or dead, businesses, companies, events, or locales is entirely coincidental.

Written by: Kate Oliver
Cover Model: Kevin Creekman

Copyright © 2023 Kate Oliver

"ALL RIGHTS RESERVED. This book contains material protected under International and Federal Copyright Laws and Treaties. Any unauthorized reprint or use of this material is prohibited. No part of this book may be reproduced or transmitted in any form or by any means, electronic or mechanical, including photocopying, recording, or by any information storage and retrieval system without express written permission from the author/publisher."

ABOUT SHADOWRIDGE GUARDIANS MC

Combining the sizzling talents of bestselling authors Pepper North, Kate Oliver, and Becca Jameson, the Shadowridge Guardians are guaranteed to give you a thrill and leave you dreaming of your own throbbing motorcycle joyride.

Are you daring enough to ride with a club of rough, growly, commanding men? The protective Daddies of the Shadowridge Guardians Motorcycle Club will stop at nothing to ensure the safety and protection of everything that belongs to them: their Littles, their club, and their town. Throw in some sassy, naughty, mischievous women who won't hesitate to serve their fair share of attitude even in the face of looming danger, and this brand new MC Romance series is ready to ignite!

Shadowridge Guardians MC
Steele
Kade
Atlas
Doc
Gabriel

ABOUT SHADOWRIDGE GUARDIANS MC

Talon
Bear
Faust
Storm

Kade

"Princess, do that again and see what happens..."

Remi is and always has been an MC baby. She's never had a choice in the matter since her dad is a member of the Shadowridge Guardians MC. But she's been avoiding the clubhouse as much as possible the past few years because every time she's near Kade Beckham she can't breathe properly, and she becomes a defensive brat toward him. When she starts getting threatening messages, though, he's the first person she calls for help.

Kade loves his club and takes pride in protecting his brothers. He would do anything for the other members or their families. That's his job after all. Enforcer. So when Remi calls him for help, he doesn't hesitate, but he also knows he needs to keep a wide distance from the prickly little goth girl. But when he finds out her secret, however, he isn't so sure he can stay away. She needs a protector and a Daddy, and he intends to be both.

She can toss that attitude all she wants, but he intends to make her his good girl.

ONE
KADE

"Hey, man. Haven't seen you in a few days."

Kade nodded toward his fellow member of the MC. "Hey, Rock. I've been busy finishing up a bike. The owner wanted it done for a show so I've been cramming."

One of the club prospects slid Kade an ice-cold beer. Nodding toward the hopeful newbie, he twisted off the cap and leaned against the bar next to Rock, motioning to the older man's chest. "How's the old ticker?"

Rock rubbed his chest and shrugged. "Still ticking."

Nodding, he took a swig from the bottle and let the fizzy liquid flow down his throat. When he lowered the beer from his mouth, he saw a movement of all black and grimaced. Remi.

"Hey, Dad," she said sweetly as she approached them.

She looked tired, something Kade had noticed the last few times he'd seen her. He knew she worked at a bar, but she usually worked the day shift, so it made him wonder if she was seeing someone who was keeping her up at night. The thought annoyed him. He didn't want to know the answer.

Remi was an MC princess. The daughter of a long-time

member, and because her mom had passed away at a young age, she'd pretty much grown up in the clubhouse. At some point in her teens, she'd gotten into the Goth phase and hadn't grown out of it, but somehow, it fit her. It wasn't a style she put on just to fit in.

Looking at the small woman, he forced himself to smile, but she completely ignored him as she smiled at her dad. She seemed to hate Kade for whatever reason, but he had no idea why.

"Hey, honey. What are you doing here?" Rock asked, wrapping his daughter up in a hug.

She hugged him back and then finally looked at Kade. Her dark eyes looked him up and down, and then she seemed to completely dismiss him as she turned to her dad. Even though she was being a prickly little thing, Kade was still worried about her not getting enough sleep. It was the Daddy in him.

"I was just heading home from work and wanted to drop you some dinner. It's a chicken breast with green beans and mashed cauliflower."

Both men grimaced.

Ever since Rock's heart attack, Remi had been making it her mission to get her dad to eat healthily, but the crap she brought him to eat was just sad. Plain, dry, and green. And what the hell was up with using cauliflower as a replacement for other things? Mashed cauliflower? Kade would rather eat dog food.

He would never say anything, but Rock almost always took the meals to a homeless person that stayed near the compound. Even though Remi seemed to hate Kade, she meant well, and he thought it was sweet that she was trying to take care of her old man.

"Dad, it's good for you," she said with a smile before she turned to Kade and glared. "And maybe you should encourage him to eat it instead of cringing along with him."

Taking another swig of his beer, he rolled his eyes, then

slapped Rock on the back. "Good luck with her, my friend. I'm heading home for the night. Night, Remi."

As he walked past her, she sidestepped, putting several feet between them as though if she got close to him, he would burn her. It shouldn't have bothered him. He shouldn't have cared what the little brat thought of him, but he did. He had a feeling it bothered him because the image of her in her black denim skirt and skin-tight black shirt with her black combat boots was the only thing he could see in his mind as he walked out to his bike.

What the fuck was wrong with him? He obviously needed to get laid, because fantasizing about his friend's daughter was basically against all bro-codes. No matter how hard he tried, though, he just couldn't seem to stop thinking about her. He'd been doing it for the past four years. Fuck. He was a terrible person.

Starting up the engine of his bike, he smiled. That sound would never get old. Neither would the wind against his skin and the vibration of the engine as he rode through the small city he called home. He hoped that by the time he got to his house, the little black-haired woman would be far away from his mind, but that didn't work out.

When he arrived, she was right there where she always was, and it drove him crazy. She'd never shown him any interest, and she sure as fuck wasn't the type of woman he normally craved. After all, he was pretty sure she wasn't the type to call any man Daddy, let alone let a man dominate and take care of her. She let her don't-fuck-with-me vibe be known to everyone.

He parked his bike in the garage and went inside his empty house, kicking off his boots before heading to the kitchen for a beer to take into the shower with him.

Once in the bathroom, he turned on the shower nozzle and waited for the temperature to warm up before he stripped out of his clothes, grabbed his beer, and stepped in. Nothing like a shower beer to unwind after a long day. Of course, there were better things to help with unwinding, but the beer would have to do for now.

His cock thickened as he started washing himself while thoughts of Remi filled his mind. He needed to stop fantasizing about her and move on with his life. She wasn't his type. Besides, she was also thirteen years younger than him. He was too damn old for her.

Ignoring his cock, he drank the beer and finished washing before he stepped out and wrapped a towel around himself. His phone rang from the pocket of the jeans he'd stripped off and discarded on the floor, so he had to search for it in the pile of clothes. He finally found it, and when he looked at the screen and saw Remi's name, he knew something was wrong.

TWO
REMI

As soon as she pulled into her parking space at her apartment complex, she let out a deep breath. She was exhausted. Not only had she not been sleeping well, but she'd been worrying nonstop. It had been five days since the last letter and it felt as though she was just waiting in fear for the next one to show up. What could she do about it, though?

She could go to the police but there weren't any threats in the letters. They were creepy as hell with declarations of love and calling her a perfect little doll. It made her skin crawl but it really wasn't enough to call the cops. And she definitely wasn't going to go to her dad. She was still so worried about him. And she wasn't calling her brother, either, because he would insist on telling their dad, so that wasn't happening.

Letting out a sigh, she got out of her car and made her way up the walkway to the front door of her apartment. She was only halfway there when she saw another envelope taped to the door. A blue envelope with her name scribbled across the front.

Her entire body started to tremble as she slowly walked the rest of the way up the path. She looked all around her, making sure no one was lurking about before she grabbed the envelope and rushed inside, locking the door behind her.

Dropping her purse on the floor, she held the envelope in her shaking hands, trying to swallow the bile rising in her throat. Tearing it open, she gasped when instead of a letter, photos fell out onto the floor at her feet. Nearly a dozen pictures. All of them were of her in her apartment, in her bedroom. Oh, God. Whoever it was knew her secret. They knew what she was, and somehow they'd gotten photos of her in her own bedroom.

Don't freak out, Remi. Don't freak out. Don't freak out.

She was totally freaking out. How could she not be? This was the fifth time someone had delivered anonymous mail. On every envelope, it said the same thing on the outside.

Remi, my little doll.

The first letter had been short and simple. Nothing particularly ominous except that it had been delivered to her apartment. The second letter was a little creepy. Details about herself that meant the person sending her the letters knew her. The third letter had her looking over her shoulder every time she was outside of her apartment because it was obvious the person was following her.

But who? Who would be that obsessed with her? Even though she worked at a bar, she only served drinks and didn't mingle with the customers other than to get their orders and give them their tabs.

But this… this was different. These were photos. Bending over, she swayed as she picked them up. She felt lightheaded. Almost feeling drunk, she walked over to the couch and sank down, dropping the pictures onto the coffee table where the other letters were sitting.

This was getting serious. Someone was truly stalking her. Not just writing letters but actually spying on her. Taking pictures through her windows. She shuddered at the thought. What all had they seen?

Her first thought was to call her dad, but his heart was still weak and the doctors told him he needed to keep his stress to a minimum. She could call Steele, the president of Shadowridge Guardians MC, but she didn't want to bother him. He was in a new relationship and she didn't want to get him involved. What if whoever was doing this was dangerous? Was she in danger?

Looking around her apartment, she jumped up from the couch and ran from window to window, pulling all the blinds closed. Were they out there right now? Watching her?

Oh, God. She dropped back down onto the couch. Sharp breaths started sawing in and out of her lungs as she tried to stop the world from going dark. She was going to have a panic attack if she didn't get control of herself.

Think, Remi. Who can you call? Who do you trust?

She knew who she trusted. She knew he would protect her even if he didn't like her. It was his job in the MC, after all. To protect the members and their families from threats. But if he saw the photos, her secret would be revealed. What would he think of her then? He'd think she was a fraud, that's what.

Looking down at the photos, her hands started to shake again. She just didn't understand why this was happening.

A hard knock on her front door practically caused her to catapult from the couch. Was that them? Shit. Did they know she was in there by herself? Of course they did. They'd taken photos of her inside her apartment. What if they were there to hurt her? Or kill her? Oh, God. She had to do something.

Getting down on all fours on the carpeted floor, she made herself as small as possible and crawled under her dining room table, pulling in the chairs to keep her enclosed in the smallest space possible. She pulled her phone from her back pocket, and opened the messenger app. She needed him. It didn't matter that he would find out the real her. He would keep her safe. It was either he find out her secret or she'd end up dead. At this point, him finding out her secret was the much more appealing option.

Not wanting to make any noise, she typed up a message as fast as she could.

> Remi: Help.
>
> Remi: I'm at my apartment.
>
> Remi: Hurry. I'm scared.
>
> Remi: Don't tell my dad.

Her fingers shook as she typed out the messages, sending one right after the other. Almost immediately, her phone started ringing and she fumbled to silence it. Hitting the answer button, she brought it up to her ear.

"Kade," she whispered.

"Remi, what's wrong?" he demanded.

She could hear rustling in the background like he was already on the move.

Holding her hand up to her mouth, she whispered as quietly as possible. "I need help. I'm scared, Kade."

"I'm coming. Do I need to bring backup?"

"No. Don't tell anyone," she sniffled. "Please, Kade."

"Remi, you're freaking me out. What the fuck is going on? Why are you whispering?"

"I don't know what's going on. I'm scared. Someone is…"

Another knock at the door made her jump and whimper.

"What was that?" he barked.

She couldn't speak. What if they heard her? What if they broke in before Kade got there? She held her hand up to her mouth to cover the sounds of her whimpering, but she couldn't get the control she wanted. She heard him start up his bike and prayed he was at his house, which was closer to her than the compound.

"I'm coming, baby girl. I'll be there soon. Stay on the phone with me."

"'Kay."

Pulling her knees up to her chest, she whimpered and listened to the soothing purr of his motorcycle through the phone. He didn't speak, but just being able to hear him, knowing he was on his way to her, helped calm her.

Minutes felt like hours, but then she heard his bike turn off.

"Can you open the door, Remi?" he asked.

"Are you outside?"

"Yeah, baby, I'm right outside."

Baby. She probably would have soaked up that little nickname if she weren't so scared out of her mind. "I'm scared."

"I know. I'm at the front door. It's just me. Open the door for me, or I'm going to kick it in."

Crawling out from under the table, she got to her feet and went to the door, rising to her toes to look out of the tiny peephole. As soon as she saw it really was Kade, she swung the door open and threw herself at him, sobbing.

His arms tightened around her and he carried her inside the apartment, kicking the door shut behind him before turning around to lock it. He set her on her feet and looked down at her with his eyebrows pulled together in concern. "Remi, what's wrong? What's going on?"

"T-they won't stop sending stuff."

He kept his hands on her biceps as he looked down at her, and the warmth of his skin on her arms soothed her more than she'd expected.

"Who, Remi? What stuff? Baby, I need to know what the fuck is going on."

Raising her shaking hand, she pointed toward the coffee

table where she'd left all the letters and photos. He looked in the direction she pointed and then back at her before he released her, went to the table, and stared down at what was there.

When he raised his gaze, his eyes were practically black, and his expression was deadly. "Who the fuck is sending this?"

THREE
KADE

He stared down at the pieces of paper and photographs in complete shock. Someone had been taking pictures of her in her apartment and sending her notes. What the fuck? And the photos weren't just random photos of her in her living room. They were pictures of her in her bedroom. In her goddamn bedroom. Rage filled him, and it took every ounce of restraint not to smash the table in front of him. The only thing stopping him from doing so was that he didn't want to scare Remi.

"When did you start getting these? Have you called the cops? Who else knows?"

She stared up at him with tears streaming down her cheeks, and he felt like an ass for firing so many questions at her while she was so upset, but he needed to know. He needed to know who he needed to kill because someone was going to pay dearly for this.

"The first one came three weeks ago. The photos came today, and then someone was knocking and I freaked out, and that's when I called you."

He looked around, trying to figure out what to do. It was obvious she wasn't safe in her apartment if they were leaving letters there. "We need to get you out of here. Pack a bag. I'm taking you to the compound."

Her eyes widened, and she started shaking her head. "I can't go to the compound. My dad can't know, Kade. He'll have another heart attack. He's still too weak to deal with extra stress."

Dammit. He hated keeping stuff from her dad. But she was right. Rock was still recovering, and Kade didn't want to be responsible for his friend ending up back in the hospital or worse.

He strode over to her. "You can't stay here, Remi. I'm either taking you to the compound or you're coming home with me. Take your pick but while you decide, go pack a bag."

When she didn't move, he grabbed hold of her arm and led her toward what he assumed was her bedroom, and he was right. Except when he walked in, he hadn't been expecting what he saw.

Pink everywhere. Her bedding, her curtains, an area rug, even her makeup vanity was pink. And the shock didn't stop there. Her bed was filled with stuffies. She probably had at least fifty of them on the full-size bed. Where the hell did she sleep?

Turning his head, he looked down and found her staring up at him with a look of shock on her face. Did she think he was going to judge her? Hell, he loved seeing her room like that. It did things to him he didn't want to think about right then. He was more surprised than anything. The dark queen was secretly a fairy princess.

"Don't you dare tell anyone that I like pink. I'll hurt you if you do," she whispered.

Narrowing his eyes toward her, he shook his head. "I would never tell your secrets. For now, pack a bag and whatever you need so you can sleep."

He motioned toward her sea of stuffies.

She lowered her dark eyes, looked over at her bed, and

then shifted her gaze back up to him. "I need all of them to be able to sleep."

If there wasn't a looming threat happening, he would have found that to be the most adorable Little thing to say, but now wasn't the time to indulge her Little side. If she even was Little. Just because she liked pink didn't mean anything. And the bed of stuffed toys didn't mean anything either. Lots of people liked to sleep with stuffed toys. Not usually that many but still, he couldn't just make assumptions… even though he absolutely was because holy fuck, he wanted her to be a Little more than he could ever remember wanting anything. "I need you to pick the most important ones for now, and I'll come back another time to get the rest. We need to get out of here. Do you need help packing?"

Her sad eyes nearly made him crumble. He knew stuffies were important but seriously? That many? She shook her head and started digging through dresser drawers.

She was almost packed up when someone knocked on the door, making her cry out and look to him with absolute terror on her face. He pulled his gun from the back of his pants and looked at her sternly. "Do not leave this room. Understand?"

Her entire body shook as she nodded. He closed her into the bedroom and went to the front door, looking out of the peephole. When he didn't see anyone out there, he slowly unlocked the door and opened it, ready to aim and fire if necessary, but he didn't see anyone. When he looked down, his blood went cold. Sitting on the doormat was a vase full of black roses. Picking up the vase, he looked it over, trying to find a card. When he found one, he brought the vase inside, making sure the front door was locked before he took it into the kitchen and set it on the counter.

Snatching the card, he ripped it open.

Black roses for my perfect little doll. I can't wait to make you mine.

He let out a low growl and slammed the card onto the counter.

"What does it say?"

Spinning around, he glared at her. "Dammit. I told you to stay in the bedroom, Remi."

Her dark eyes moved from the card up to his gaze. "I heard you shut and lock the door. What does the card say, Kade?"

Kade stomped over to her, stopped just inches away, and lowered his face to hers so he was at eye level with her. "I don't care what you heard. If I tell you to do something, especially in regard to your safety, you do it. I can't protect you if you don't obey me. Do something like that again and you won't sit for a week. Got it?"

She stared at him for a long moment before she slowly nodded. Yeah, he was being an ass. He knew he was being an ass, but the one girl he'd cared about in years was being threatened by some stalker, and he would do whatever was necessary to protect her, including spanking her ass if that's what it took to get her to obey him.

"Fine," she snapped.

FOUR
REMI

So many things were going on at once, and she was about to have a meltdown. She couldn't handle it all. Not only was Kade being a jerk and bossing her around, but there was a stalker leaving stuff on her doorstep. Twice in one day. And when Kade had left her alone in her bedroom, she'd panicked. Now her only option was to either go home with Kade or go to the compound where her dad lived. She could not go to the club. Her dad was still too weak for this kind of stress.

Kade straightened. "We need to go."

Feeling too tired to argue, she let him lead her back to her bedroom where she had as many belongings packed into a bag as she could get. Without hesitating, Kade grabbed the pink bag and led her back out to the living room where he grabbed the letters and photos and stuffed them into the pocket of his cut.

Running his fingers through his hair, he looked around. "Need anything else?"

She shook her head and grabbed her black purse, which was also a mini backpack with bat wings on it, and followed him to the front door.

He turned and looked down at her. "I'm going to follow you on my bike. Do you remember where I live?"

"Yes."

Of course she remembered. She'd gone there once with her dad. She'd also driven past his house a time or two on purpose because... well, she didn't know why. He was Kade. He was the hottest guy she'd ever known, and he was a Daddy. The only problem was he was a lot older than her and hadn't known she was a Little. Although it was hard to deny now that he'd seen her bedroom.

"Stay by my side until you're in the car and then lock your doors as soon as you get in."

He pulled his gun from the waistband of his jeans and opened the front door, looking all around before he let her through the doorway. She felt as though she was being escorted by a security guard. Well, she kind of was.

Before they made it to her car, Kade let out a string of curse words, and when she looked up at him and noticed him looking at something, she followed his line of sight, letting out a gasp. Both tires on his motorcycle were flat and one of them was visibly slashed. Looking back at him, she felt her bottom lip quiver as tears threatened to spill over again.

"Oh, my gosh, Kade, I'm sorry. It's all my fault."

He shook his head and started walking again. "It's not your fault, Princess. It's whoever's doing this, and they have no fucking clue who they're dealing with."

He walked her around to the passenger side of her black sedan, opened the door for her, made sure she was in safe, and then went around to the driver's side and got in. She handed him the keys, thankful she didn't have to drive because honestly, she probably couldn't have handled driving right then.

As soon as he pulled out of her apartment complex, she burst into tears. "I'm sorry, Kade. I didn't know who else to call, and I don't know who's doing this. I was just so scared, and what if they want to hurt me?"

He continued to drive as he reached over and took her hand in his, squeezing it gently. "You called the right person. I'm going to protect you. It's going to be okay. Da— I'm here, I got you."

Even though she was practically hysterical, she didn't miss what he'd almost said. He'd almost called himself Daddy. And even though he corrected himself, she still pretended that he'd said it because right then, that's what she needed. A Daddy. Not just any Daddy, though. She needed Kade.

"What are you going to do about your motorcycle?"

She could see his jaw flexing and knew he was trying to keep his cool over it. But messing with an MC member's motorcycle? Specifically, the enforcer? That was just a death wish.

"I'm going to call one of my employees at the shop to pick it up."

Her eyes widened. "But they'll tell my dad or Steele. I don't want people to know—"

"Your dad isn't going to find out. I won't let that happen. Trust me, okay?"

She did trust him. She trusted him with her life, which was why he was the one she'd reached out to instead of anyone else. He was loyal to his club, and he would protect any member or family member with his life. "I trust you."

He squeezed her hand. "Thank you, Princess."

Rolling her eyes, she turned to look at him. "If you ever call me princess in front of anyone, I'll hurt you."

His deep laugh warmed her from the inside out. "Whatever you say, Princess."

Well, crap. She hoped she'd packed enough pairs of panties because if she was going to be around him, staying at his house, she would need to change them frequently.

She studied him as he drove. His shoulder-length dirty

blond hair was disheveled but it looked sexy on him, and every time he ran his fingers through it, her mouth dried up like the desert. Ever since she'd hit puberty, she'd had a crush on Kade. She was sure every single woman in town crushed over him, though. Heck, maybe even the married women too. He had the whole sexy tattooed biker look down, and the best part was, he was an actual biker who got his hands dirty working on customizing motorcycles all day. She wondered how those rough, callused hands would feel on her body and suddenly felt warm. Yeah, she was going to need to keep her thoughts and fantasies in check. It wasn't like he was into her. He was just doing a good deed.

When they got to his house and went inside, he looked over at her and smiled. "Welcome home for the time being."

Offering him a tight smile, she nodded. "Thanks. I'll try to stay out of your way."

"You won't be in my way, Remi. But there will be rules I expect you to follow."

Swallowing heavily, she looked up at him. "Super."

He shot her a look. "Come on. Let's get you settled. You can sleep in my room. I don't have any beds set up in the guest rooms yet, so I'll sleep on the couch."

Holy hell. There was no way she was sleeping in his bed. She'd never fall asleep for one. For two, she'd be in a constant state of arousal because his bed would surely smell like him. And for three, she wasn't going to take his bed away from him. "I'll sleep on the couch. I'm smaller."

The stern look he gave her had her fidgeting.

"You will sleep in my bed. End of discussion."

Her mouth fell open. Well... Okay. Guess she would be sleeping in his bed.

FIVE
KADE

He took her bag into his bedroom and set it on the chair in the corner of the room. His house was nothing special, but it was his, and when he needed some solitude away from his MC brothers, that's where he was. He spent about half his time staying at the club and half his time at his house, but with Remi there, he would be there all the time. He wouldn't be leaving her side until he figured out what the hell was going on. And figuring that out would be more of a challenge since he'd promised not to tell anyone about it.

His mind went back to her pink bedroom, and the more he thought about it, he was pretty sure she was a Little. But why had she threatened to hurt him if he told anyone she liked pink? Most of the men that belonged to the MC were Daddies. Hell, even her dad had been a Daddy to her mom before she'd passed away. None of the men kept it a secret about who they were, so why was she so worried about revealing who she was if that's what she was?

Knowing it was actually possible she was a Little was going to be torture. He'd already thought about Remi nonstop for the past four years, but because she was Rock's daughter, he'd always known she was off-limits, and it had been a little easier to keep his distance when the only side he knew of her was the dark, prickly side. But now... all he wanted to do was claim her as his and Daddy the hell out of her. She didn't seem to feel the same way, even though it had been pretty damn cute that she'd threatened him bodily harm if he called her princess in front of anyone.

As he turned around to leave his room, he stopped in his tracks when he found Remi standing in the doorway, looking up at him with her dark lined eyes. He wondered what she would look like with her face scrubbed free of all her dark makeup. Then again, she always did a good job on her makeup, and he knew she would be gorgeous either way.

"Make yourself at home. Give me a list of groceries and I'll order them to be delivered. Do not leave this house without me, understand? Until I know what the fuck is going on, you're on lockdown with me, okay?"

She pulled her bottom lip between her teeth as she stared up at him, and he had to force himself not to reach up and pluck that plump lip free with his thumb.

"I don't have a shift at The Hangout today or tomorrow, but I'll have to go to work after that. And you have to work too."

He hated that she worked in a bar. Not that there was anything wrong with the job itself, he just didn't like that she was there getting hit on all the time. The thought of it made him want to punch something. And he knew it happened all the time because he'd seen it happen when he'd been there with some of the guys before.

"I'll take a few days off. You will too. We need to stay low while I try to figure this out, but Remi, I need to tell Steele at least. You know he won't judge you for being Little."

Her shoulders sagged and she walked over to his bed and sat on the edge, making his cock thicken in his jeans. The sight of her on his bed was too damn inviting. He had to look away and silently count to ten to get himself under control.

"I'm not Little."

If she'd kept her eyes on him or not lowered her voice when she'd said it, he might have believed her.

"Yes, you are. Don't lie to me."

Shooting her gaze up to his, she stared at him for a long moment before she let out a deep sigh. "You're such a jerk sometimes," she murmured. "People will think I'm a fraud. I mean, I wear all black but I secretly love pink. They'll think I'm some sort of freak."

He walked over to the bed and sat down beside her. "No one is going to think that, Remi. There are so many people out there who are totally different day to day from how they are when they're Little. There is no right or wrong way to be Little. I've met women who are high-powered businesswomen and when they get home from work, they strip off that side of them and become the Littlest Littles there are."

Her eyes narrowed at him. "How do you know them?"

The question surprised him. Why did she care? "Are you jealous, Princess?"

Dropping her mouth open, she scoffed. "What? No!"

He grinned and leaned his shoulder into hers. "And here, all this time, I thought you hated me."

She froze and looked up at him. "I never hated you. I thought you didn't like me. That you thought I was just some dumb kid."

Furrowing his eyebrows, he shook his head. "I haven't seen you as a kid for years, Remi. I think it was your twenty-first birthday when I realized you were definitely not a kid anymore."

Her eyes widened as she stared up at him, and before he realized what he was doing, he lowered his face so they were only inches apart. She let out a soft sigh, pulling him back to reality. Shit. He needed to be careful. She was his friend's daughter.

Leaning back, he cleared his throat and stood. "I'm going to go find something to make us for dinner. Unpack and get comfortable."

Then he hightailed it out of his bedroom before he lost control.

SIX
REMI

Her body was buzzing as she watched Kade leave the room. Had he just been about to kiss her? No, of course not. He didn't like her like that. She was way younger than him. He was just helping her because she was a family member of the MC. It wasn't like they were even friends.

Looking around, she took in his room. It was definitely a bachelor pad, but it was clean and comfortable. Flopping back on the bed, she sighed. He knew about her Little side. And her pink bedroom. How embarrassing.

She thought about his comment about noticing on her twenty-first birthday that she was an adult. What had he meant by that? Kade was a Daddy, though up until tonight, he hadn't known she was Little.

Nibbling on her bottom lip, she resisted the urge to dig Binks out of her backpack. She could really use the comfort. It felt as though she had nine million things going through her mind all at once. She had a stalker. Kade found out she was Little. He saw her pink room. Her stalker had slashed Kade's tires.

Suddenly her breathing was coming in sharp pants, and it

felt as though her lungs were on fire. Shit. She was having a panic attack. Pulling herself up to sit, she leaned forward and put her head in her hands, trying to remind herself to breathe. Tears filled her eyes as she fought through it, but she couldn't stop the sob that broke free.

Within seconds, Kade was kneeling in front of her, both his hands wrapped around her wrists. "Breathe, baby. Deep breath in and then out. Good girl. You're safe. I'm right here. In, out. Good girl."

She followed his commands even though it felt like her chest was on fire with each breath she took.

"Breathe again, baby. Good girl."

His deep voice soothed her, and without thinking, she reached out and ran her fingers over his jaw, feeling the roughness of his short beard. Her breathing became more even, but she could feel a fine layer of sweat on her skin, and she could barely keep her eyes open. Panic attacks always exhausted her.

Kade stood and lifted her from the bed, and while she should have probably told him to put her down, she didn't because it felt good to be held against him. He carried her into the bathroom and set her on the counter, keeping one hand on her thigh while he grabbed a washcloth from a drawer and then ran it under water.

He brought the cloth up to her forehead and she sighed. It was cool and soothing, and when she reached up to take it from him, he grabbed hold of her wrist and brought her hand back to her lap.

"Let me take care of you."

She stared at him as he concentrated on what he was doing. "Thank you, Kade."

Lowering his hand, he studied her with those deep green eyes that made her melt. "How often do you have panic attacks?"

"Not very often. Lately I've been having them more. Ever since I started getting the letters."

He moved in front of her, placing his hands on either side of the counter, trapping her in. Pinning her with a stern look, he asked, "Why didn't you call me sooner?"

"I thought about it but I didn't want my dad to find out. And I didn't think you liked me."

Moving his face down so it was only inches from hers, he held her gaze. "Well, get that out of your head because I do like you."

"But you've always kept your distance from me and you barely speak to me."

Taking a step back, he shook his head. "That's because you always seemed to be hissing at me whenever I was around."

"I was not hissing!"

Raising an eyebrow, he smirked. "You're hissing right now, Princess."

Crossing her arms over her chest, she stuck her lip out in a pout. "Am not."

He took a step forward again and placed his hands back on the counter. "Well, for the record, I do like you, Remi. I fucking like you a lot. But your dad is my friend and I don't want to make a move on his daughter and ruin our friendship. I respect him too much."

She didn't know why he would think her dad wouldn't approve of him. Her dad loved Kade. "It wouldn't hurt your friendship."

Keeping his gaze on hers, he raised an eyebrow. "You didn't say you didn't want me to make a move on you."

Reaching up, she grabbed hold of the edges of his cut. "That's because maybe I want you to."

His pupils dilated, and she could tell that he was rolling that little piece of information around in his mind.

"You know my life is crazy, Remi. You deserve better than that. You deserve better than me. You deserve roses and sunshine."

Her lips pulled back into a smile. She gestured to her all

black outfit. "Do I look like I'm a roses and sunshine kind of girl?"

He grinned. "The secret part of you seems like you're a roses and sunshine kind of girl."

Shrugging, she leaned forward and rested her head on his shoulder. His hand instantly came up to the back of her head, stroking her hair.

He sighed. "Let's go eat dinner."

She nodded and before she could hop off the counter, he lifted her and set her down on her feet and then placed his hand on her lower back and led her out of the bedroom toward the kitchen.

When he pulled out a chair for her at the small dining table, she smiled up at him. She hated that he didn't see how sweet and wonderful he was. He was the man who would give the shirt off his back just to help someone in need. That was the kind of man she wanted. Roses meant nothing to her.

"I made your favorite."

He placed a plate of spaghetti casserole in front of her, making her squeal. "I can't believe you remembered my favorite food."

His cheeks turned a light shade of pink and he shrugged like it meant nothing. "Eat up, Princess."

This time it was her cheeks that turned pink. Why did she like him calling her that so much? It was strange because she'd liked him for so long and fantasized about him hundreds of times but she'd never thought he'd liked her like that. Now, knowing that he did and hearing him call her baby and princess, yeah, that was even better than she could have ever imagined.

SEVEN
KADE

He watched her eat her dinner and inwardly groaned every time she made one of those cute little noises that told him just how much she liked it. He was no chef, but he could throw together a good meal and spaghetti casserole just happened to be the one meal he excelled at. They would eat spaghetti casserole every night if it meant he got to hear those seductive noises.

Forcing his mind to focus on something other than wanting to strip her naked and lick every inch of her, Kade cleared his throat. "Has anyone been acting strange toward you? At the bar or at the MC or anything like that?"

She furrowed her eyebrows. "You know that no one at the MC would hurt me."

He shrugged. He wasn't so sure about that. For some reason, he just didn't trust one particular member. It was just a feeling and he had no proof but the club treasurer had been acting strange recently. The guy was dating Remi's best friend, Carlee, though, so that wouldn't make sense. "What about at the bar? Any guys creeping you out?"

Shrugging her shoulders, she twirled her fork in the

noodles. "There's always guys that ask me out. It's a bar. But nothing out of the ordinary."

Kade let out a low growl. He didn't fucking like that. Guys hitting on his girl? Hell, no.

Dude, she's not your girl. Chill.

"Now who's jealous?" she asked with raised brows.

"Eat your dinner," he muttered.

She giggled and rolled her eyes but she took a bite and moaned appreciatively. He was going to have to take a cold shower after she went to bed, otherwise he was going to be in pain all night.

He could tell she was exhausted from her panic attack, and all he wanted to do when they were done eating was strip her naked, give her a bath, and then put her to bed, but they weren't there yet. And they may never be. As badly as he wanted her, which was pretty damn bad, he didn't want to do anything to rock the boat in the MC. Even if she was the first girl he'd ever imagined marrying.

Instead of doing what he wanted to do, he took their dishes to the sink. "Why don't you go get some pajamas on?"

"I'll help with the dishes. You cooked," she said softly.

He turned around and smiled down at her as she walked toward him. "You're exhausted, and you've been through a lot today. Go get comfy. Do you want to take a bath before you get your pajamas on?"

Her cheeks turned pink as she lowered her gaze from his. Was she thinking the same thing as he had been? She lifted up on her toes and fidgeted. Was her Little side peeking out? Finally she shook her head. "Can I take a quick shower?"

Walking over to her, he cupped her chin and studied her face. "Are you feeling okay? I don't want you to get in the shower if you're too tired."

"I'm okay. I'm really tired, but I just feel icky after everything that happened today."

"Okay, Princess. Leave the bathroom door cracked and call out for me if you start feeling like you're panicking. Got it?"

"Okay," she murmured before she disappeared into the hall bathroom.

A few minutes later, he heard the water running and he busied himself with the dishes so he wouldn't think about the fact that Remi was in his guest bathroom, stripping her clothes off.

When the kitchen was clean, he shut off the light and went into his bedroom to find some pajamas for himself. Grabbing a pair of sweats and a T-shirt, he headed into the attached bathroom and changed. Remi was standing by his bed when he opened the door, and he paused to look at her.

He'd known her for her entire life, but he couldn't remember the last time he'd seen her bare-faced, and there she was with not a trace of makeup on her skin. She turned to look at him, her dark brown eyes traveling up his body until she met his gaze. She took his breath away. Her skin was so creamy and smooth, and her long dark lashes lined her wide eyes perfectly. She looked so innocent. So adorable. And the pink pajama set she was wearing was just the cherry on top.

"It's strange seeing you in pink."

Her lips pulled back into a soft smile. "Do you think I'm weird?"

Walking over to her, he brushed a wet strand of hair away from her face. "No. I think you're perfect. I won't say I'm not surprised because I am. I never expected this side of you but it's a good surprise."

He wanted to ask her so many questions. How old was her Little? What did she like to do when she was in that headspace? Did she like sippy cups and pacifiers? He considered asking her all of that, but when she swayed slightly, he realized those questions would have to wait because she needed to go to sleep.

He went over to his bed and pulled the blankets back. "I

just changed the sheets yesterday but I can change them again if you want."

She shook her head and climbed up onto the mattress. "No. I'm fine. Thank you. But I really don't mind sleeping on the couch. You'll be so uncomfortable."

"I'll be just fine. You saw how big my couch is. Besides, there's no way in hell I'm letting you be between me and the front door. I'll always be the one who's between you and danger. Now, do you need anything before you go to sleep?"

"Can you hand me my bag?"

He went over to the chair, grabbed her bag, and brought it to her, watching as she dug through it and then looked up at him shyly before pulling out a small stuffed bat and a teddy bear. Not just any teddy bear, either. It was the teddy bear he'd given her when her dad had been in the hospital and he'd found her crying in the hallway. That had been one of the only times she'd let down her guard around him and let him hug her. Up until now, at least.

"You kept him."

She nodded and clutched the bear to her chest. "He's one of my favorite stuffies. You gave him to me when I was the most sad I could ever remember being, and it cheered me up. He and Binks are my two favorites. Although I love all my stuffies."

He watched her turn animated as she told him about her stuffies, and he knew her Little side was showing. It was the sweetest thing he'd ever witnessed. "Who is Binks?"

Her bare cheeks turned bright pink as she held up the stuffed bat. Of course, his little Goth girl would have a stuffed bat. It fit her perfectly.

"He's cute."

Giggling, she shook her head. "Binks is a girl, silly."

Oh, yeah, her Little was there, and it was freaking adorable. And if he didn't leave the room soon, he was going to tuck her in, kiss her forehead, and then it would be impossible to leave her, so instead, he smiled and nodded. "Silly me. Get some rest, Princess. I'll be out in the living room if you need anything."

She slid down under the covers and pulled both stuffies under with her. "Night, Kade."

"Night, Remi."

"Kade," she whispered.

He turned and looked at her from the doorway. "Yeah?"

"Thank you."

"You're welcome, baby girl. Night."

EIGHT
REMI

She couldn't sleep. Every time she closed her eyes, she kept seeing those letters and photographs. Who would do such a thing? And if that person had been taking photos of her from right outside her apartment, had they been inside her apartment at some point without her knowing? A shiver coursed through her and suddenly, she was on her feet with her teddy bear dangling from her hand as she made her way out to the living room.

The house was dark except for the dim light of the hallway bathroom, which she guessed he'd left on for her benefit since she was pretty sure Kade wasn't scared of the dark. Neither was she. Not really anyway. Okay, maybe just a little. Especially right then when her mind was going crazy thinking about everything.

As soon as she stepped into the living room, she heard Kade move.

"What's wrong, Princess?"

She hated that she woke him, but she was scared, and she was afraid to fall asleep because she didn't want to have nightmares. "I'm sorry to wake you."

With her eyes adjusted to the dark, she could see him sit up on the couch.

"Come here," he said softly.

Walking over to him, she let him pull her down onto the couch next to him. His arms wrapped around her, and she realized he wasn't wearing a shirt. It wasn't like she hadn't seen him without a shirt before, but she'd never touched his bare chest. It was both comforting and arousing at the same time.

He held her firmly, and she instantly relaxed against him. Compared to her, Kade was enormous. He was over six feet tall and muscular. He looked like he worked out every day when in reality she was pretty sure he got all his muscles from working in his motorcycle shop.

"Did you have a bad dream?"

She shook her head. "No. I never fell asleep. Every time I try, I keep thinking about those letters and photos. I just don't understand. Why would someone be doing this?"

His hand moved up to her head as she rested it on his shoulder, and he started stroking her hair. "I don't know, baby. You're safe with me, though. I'm not going to let anyone hurt you."

Yeah, she knew that. Kade would protect her with his own life. "I know. You're so good to everyone in the MC."

He stilled his hand. "I'm not protecting you just because you're MC family. I'm protecting you because I care about you, Remi. I always have."

Letting out a sigh, she nodded and clutched her bear tighter. She cared about him too. It was weird being the center of his attention because she'd always stayed in the background and she'd always thought he was avoiding her, so she'd only been able to know him from a distance.

Kade shifted and stood, pulling her up into his arms. She reached up and looped her arm around his neck. "What are you doing?"

"I'm taking you to bed."

Her bottom lip trembled. "I don't want to be alone."

His arms tightened. "I'm not leaving you alone. I'll stay with you."

Oh. Well, that was nice. Wait, was he going to stay in bed with her? Or was he going to sit in the chair in the corner of the room? She didn't have to wait long to find out because as soon as he set her down on the bed, he slid in next to her and tucked his arm under her neck, pulling her into him.

Her face was so close to his chest that even in the dim lighting, she could trace her finger along the lines of his tattoos. "Kade?"

"Yeah, baby?"

"You smell good. Kind of edible."

He let out a low, throaty groan. "Go to sleep before you kill me, Princess."

A slow smile spread across her face, and she was glad he couldn't see her in the dark because she was pretty sure her cheeks were the color of rubies. And if she were feeling just a little more bold, she probably would have slid her hand under the sheets to see if she would find something hard under there, but she wasn't feeling bold. She was feeling Little and safe, which made her very sleepy.

Letting out a soft sigh, she closed her eyes and snuggled into his chest, and within seconds, she shifted into a peaceful dreamland.

Remi woke with the need to void her bladder, but she was so warm and comfortable in her bed that she didn't want to move. Then she remembered she wasn't in her bed. She was in

Kade's bed, and based on the hand stroking her bicep, she wasn't alone.

Shifting onto her back, she rolled right into Kade's chest, making her eyes pop open. He was looking down at her and holy shit. Morning Kade was freaking sexy. His normally tousled hair was even more messy, and his five-o'clock shadow was filling in, making him look scruffy but in a "doing it on purpose" kind of way. When he slowly smiled, she realized she was staring and raised her eyes to his.

"Morning."

Oh, God, even his voice was deeper and had that gravelly thing going on. She couldn't stop herself from squeezing her thighs together. "Hi."

Hi? Smooth, Remi.

"You seemed to sleep well once I tucked you in and got into bed with you."

Oh, great, they were going to start the morning off with her blushing. "Yeah. I did. Thank you."

He winked at her. "Wasn't really a hardship on my part, Princess."

Squeezing her thighs again, she remembered that she still needed to use the bathroom and scrambled to try to get out of bed. He tightened his arm around her, not letting her move. "Where are you going?"

Giggling, she brought her hands to her face, trying to hide how flushed he was making her. "I need to go to the bathroom."

Lifting his arm off of her, he chuckled. "Okay, go potty. Don't want you having an accident, although Daddies have ways of dealing with that if needed."

Letting out a small squeak, she practically flung herself off the bed and hurried to the bathroom, closing the door behind her. She wasn't sure if she wanted to know what he meant by having ways of dealing with accidents. After using the toilet, she washed her hands and opened the top drawer, hoping to find a tube of toothpaste since hers was in the other bathroom from the night before. Score. Grabbing the tube, she squirted some onto her finger and did the best job she could of finger-brushing her teeth so she wouldn't have morning breath if he got close to her.

When she stepped out of the bathroom, Kade was nowhere to be seen. She went to her bag and found some clean panties, a bra, a pair of black ripped skinny jeans, and a black band T-shirt, then grabbed her makeup bag and went back into the bathroom.

Just as she was pulling her pajama shorts down her legs, Kade walked in, making her scream and lose her balance. Before she hit the floor, he rushed in and grabbed her, swooping her up off her feet.

"Kade! I was changing."

He shrugged. "So? You've seen me without a shirt."

Biting her bottom lip, she lowered her gaze to his naked chest and then looked up at him again. He grinned at her and set her down on her feet. "Why are you changing?"

"Because it's daytime and I'm in my pajamas."

Leaning a hip against the bathroom counter, he crossed his thick arms over his chest. "We aren't going anywhere. Stay in your pajamas."

She grinned. "You just like seeing me in pink."

Chuckling, he nodded. "I do. But I like seeing you in all black too. You're adorable both ways."

Her cheeks turned pink. "Flirt."

He studied her for a long moment, and she knew she wasn't going to like what he was about to say.

"I want to tell Steele about what's going on. I know you don't want your dad to find out, and I promise he won't, but if there is someone threatening you, it could be a threat to the club, and there are other women and Littles associated with the club that need to be protected. You know you can trust Steele too."

Crap. He was right and she'd never be able to forgive herself if another woman got hurt because she didn't want anyone to know about her Little side. It wasn't as if Steele wouldn't understand. He was a Daddy too and he had a Little girl of his own who Remi adored. Letting out a sigh, she nodded. "Okay."

NINE
KADE

He left Remi in the bathroom to change while he sent Steele a text, asking him to come by. Going to the compound wasn't an option since Rock would most likely be there and have questions as to why the two of them were showing up together.

When she came into the living room, she was dressed in a pair of black ripped skinny jeans, a black band T-shirt, and she had her usual black winged eyeliner on, accentuating her dark eyes. Her long black hair was straightened and hanging loose around her shoulders. It was a drastic transformation from the woman he'd seen a few minutes ago, but she was still just as perfect. She had her sketchbook in one hand and she seemed nervous as she looked around the room.

"Steele is on his way."

She nodded and sat down on the couch, pulling her feet up under her. He watched as she opened the sketchbook and started drawing, pausing every few seconds to examine what she'd drawn and then erase what she didn't want.

Leaving her to continue her sketch, he went into his bedroom, pulled the photos and letters from the pocket of his cut, and took them out to the kitchen, laying them out on the center island just as there was a knock at the door.

Pulling his gun from the back of his jeans, he went to the door and looked out the peephole before tucking his gun away. Opening the door, he nodded to Steele and then smiled down at Ivy, who was bouncing on her toes.

"Hey, Ivy."

The Little girl beamed up at him. "Hey, Kade."

Steele and Ivy stared up at him expectantly, and he knew they were waiting for him to invite them inside. "Before you come in, you should know that Remi is here."

Ivy squealed, bending to the side to try to look around him while Steele's eyebrows pulled together in confusion.

"Her dad can't find out," he added.

Steele tilted his head. "What's going on, Kade?"

Motioning for the couple to come inside, he sighed. "Come in and we'll explain."

"I knew it. I just knew it, Daddy," Ivy whispered to Steele.

Shaking his head, Steele tapped his Little girl's bottom. "Hush, Little girl. You don't know anything until they confirm it."

Letting out a sigh, Ivy skipped into the house, pulling Steele with her as Kade followed. As soon as Ivy saw Remi, she let go of her Daddy's hand and skipped over to the couch, plopping down next to her friend.

Steele crossed his arms over his chest and looked at Remi and then to Kade. "Explain."

Grabbing the photos and letters from the counter, Kade took them to Steele and handed them to him. Steele was the president of the Shadowridge Guardians, and on top of that, Kade had known him all his life. They were like family and he trusted the man with his life just as Steele trusted Kade with his.

He stared at his friend while he read the letters, his eyes getting darker with each passing second. The men took protecting women very seriously and especially vulnerable Littles. As Steele studied the photos, Kade knew he was putting two and two together that Remi was a Little.

"What's he reading?" Ivy asked.

Kade looked over at the two women. Remi was chewing on her bottom lip while Ivy looked from Kade to Steele and then back at Kade with a worried expression.

When Steele finally looked up, his gaze zeroed in on Remi. "Do you have any idea who's sending this stuff?"

She shook her head. "No."

"When did all of this start?" Steele asked.

"About three weeks ago," she said so quietly that Kade barely heard her.

Steele looked like he was ready to explode, but he was keeping a tight rein on his temper. "Why am I just now finding out about this?"

Kade sighed. "Because I just found out about it last night when she called me. They dropped off the pictures yesterday, and then while I was at her place, someone knocked on the door and when I opened it, there were black roses on the doorstep with a note. My tires were slashed on my bike too."

Ivy gasped and grabbed hold of Remi's hand while Steele started pacing, letting out a string of curse words.

"You can't tell my dad. He's too weak still. That's why I didn't tell anyone. I'm sorry, you guys."

Both men pinned her with a stern look.

"Remi, you're our family. You know that. You should have come to us as soon as the first letter came. I understand you don't want your dad to know but goddammit, you could have been hurt. And I don't understand why you felt the need to keep your Little side a secret because you know we would never judge you. We love you, Remi girl," Steele scolded.

She sank down farther into the couch and nodded, looking up at Kade with wide eyes and then to Steele. "I know. I'm sorry."

Sighing, Steele ran a hand over his face. "You guys need to come stay at the compound. There's more security there."

Remi's eyes immediately widened, but before she could protest, Kade had an idea. "Can we send Rock on a job so we can get her to the compound without being seen? She can stay in my apartment. No one would go in there."

Steele nodded. "That's a good idea. I actually need to get my new classic car to Seattle so Hawk can work on it now that he's done with yours. I can ask him to take a prospect with him."

Looking over at Remi, Kade nodded. "I think Steele is right, Princess. You'll be safer, and your dad won't even know you're there."

Ivy's eyes widened to the size of saucers as she looked from Remi to Kade and then back to Remi again. Only Remi was now glaring at Kade.

"I told you not to call me that in front of people," she hissed.

Fuck. She had. Although he hadn't really thought she'd meant it. It had just sort of slipped out. It came so natural to him for some reason.

"Are you two—?" Ivy started to ask.

"Ivy," Steele said in a low, stern voice that had Ivy clamping her mouth shut.

"She's mine," Kade said without even thinking.

This time, Remi's eyes turned wide as saucers. Steele walked over to Ivy and held out his hand for her. "Come on, Emerald Eyes, we should probably go and let these two figure out whatever seems to need to be figured out. I'll text you when Rock leaves the compound."

Kade nodded but he didn't move his gaze off Remi. He couldn't tell if she wanted to claw his eyes out, jump on him, or laugh in his face.

Steele and Ivy let themselves out without another word while he continued to keep his gaze on hers. When she opened her mouth to say something, he shook his head and walked over to her, lowering himself onto the coffee table across from her.

"You're mine, Princess. I don't know how it's going to go with your dad, but I know that you're mine and I'm going to protect you. Got it?"

TEN
REMI

What was it about a man declaring you're his that was so damn hot? She almost felt the need to fan herself, but she was in too much shock to do anything. Instead, she gaped at him because that's just how smooth she was.

"I asked you a question, Remi Lynn. Do you understand what I just said?"

Slowly, she nodded and closed her mouth to wet her tongue before she started asking questions. "All this time I thought you didn't like me and now you're saying I'm yours? You just found out I was Little yesterday. How can you even be sure? Are you only saying that so I'll sleep with you?"

Kade's expression turned dark, causing a shiver to run down her spine. One thing about Kade was that while he was hot as sin and women practically drooled over the sight of him, he was also one scary-looking guy sometimes. He looked like the kind of guy who could rip someone to shreds and then attend a birthday party for a toddler right afterward like nothing had ever happened. She wasn't afraid of him, though. She knew deep down that Kade was a good man and that he would never harm a hair on her head. But the way he was looking at her right then made her fidget.

He reached out and cupped her chin firmly. "First of all, Princess, I know you're mine because I've felt something for you since your twenty-first birthday, but I also had no clue you were Little, and I knew that if I tried to suppress my Daddy side in a relationship, I wouldn't be happy because I thrive on control. Second, not only do I want to sleep with you, I want to spread you open on my bed and eat your pussy until you're screaming my name, and then I want to fill your pussy with my cock and come deep inside you. But even if sex was completely off the table, you'd still be my Little girl and I'd still be your Daddy because I can feel it deep in my bones that you are meant for me."

Whew. Okay, she really did need to fan herself or take a cold shower or something because the room was suddenly hot, and it felt like her skin was flushed all over.

Kade tightened his hold on her chin. "Now, any other questions or arguments?"

She shook her head as much as his hand would allow, and as soon as she did, his mouth crashed onto hers. She froze at first, surprised by his kiss, but she quickly started kissing him back, moaning into his mouth as he explored hers with his tongue. His fingers were threaded in her hair, holding on tightly so he was in complete control. Squeezing her thighs together, she whimpered when he nipped at her bottom lip and pulled back to stare into her eyes. Her body went from warm to feeling like an inferno.

"I'm glad we cleared that up. We need to get ready to head to the compound but when we get there, we're going to go over rules and limits. Okay?"

Suddenly, she felt very Little and painfully turned on. Thankfully, they had to get ready to go to the compound, so she was able to try to sort her thoughts. By the time they got the text from Steele that Rock was gone, her thoughts were still a jumbled mess, and she had to sneak off to the bathroom to change her wet panties.

Her phone buzzed with a text from Ivy.

> Ivy: I'm so excited you're coming to the compound! We can play together. You know, if you want to. I understand if you don't. I've just never had any Little friends. I know Carlee is Little but she hasn't been around lately so I haven't gotten the chance to play with her.

Biting her bottom lip, Remi typed back a message.

> Remi: I'd love to play. You don't think I'm weird because I wear all black but I secretly love pink?
>
> Ivy: Not at all. I think it's so cool.

She reread Ivy's message about Carlee not being around. Remi had been so stressed out about her own situation that she hadn't really noticed how little she and Carlee had been talking. She felt like a terrible friend. Once they got settled at the compound, she would text Carlee and check on her. She knew her friend had started dating the Shadowridge Guardians' treasurer, Silver, so Carlee was probably just wrapped up in her own new relationship. How cool would it be if both she and Carlee found their Daddies in the MC?

"Let's go, Princess."

She looked up to find Kade standing in the doorway to his bedroom with a backpack slung over one shoulder. He ran his fingers through his tousled blond hair, and she could swear that move alone made her mouth go dry. She giggled at the mental image of the two of them together: MC biker and Goth princess.

He quirked an eyebrow and looked at her with a half-smile. "What's so funny?"

Shrugging, she grabbed her bag and went to walk past him in the doorway, but he stopped her and took her bag out of her hands.

"Little girls don't carry heavy things. That's their Daddy's job."

A shiver ran through her. He was her Daddy. Holy hell. How did that even happen? It happened so damn fast her head was spinning. His half-smile widened as he watched her react to his words. Ducking her head, she slid past him, hearing his chuckle behind her as they made their way out of the house.

As soon as they were outside, playful Kade was gone and enforcer Kade was very present as he looked everywhere while leading her to the passenger side of her car. He tossed their bags into the back seat and then leaned in her door and pulled the seatbelt over her. While she was on edge because of his sudden alertness, her body reacted to his chest brushing against her nipples as he reached over her.

The moment was over in a blink as he closed the door and rounded the front of the car while still looking at all his surroundings. Neither of them spoke during the drive, and when she realized he'd taken several unnecessary turns, she looked over at him and noticed he kept looking in the rearview mirror. "What's wrong?"

Not moving his eyes off the road, he handed her his phone. "Call Steele and give me the phone."

His tone was sharp, giving no room for argument or questions. Taking the device from him, she started to tremble as she hurried to find Steele's name. As soon as she pressed the call button, she handed the phone to him.

"There's a black truck following us. It looks like a Dodge of some kind. Can you get guys out there?"

Remi spun around in her seat to try to look at the truck he was talking about.

"Turn around, Little girl," he demanded.

Turning back around, she looked at him wide-eyed as he listened to whatever Steele was saying on the phone.

"Yeah. We're about seven minutes away. The truck is still following."

He pulled the phone from his ear and dropped it into one of the cup holders. Her entire body shook and it felt like her skin was ice cold as she stared at him, unable to speak.

Looking over at her, he grabbed hold of one of her hands. "It's okay, Princess. Just breathe for Daddy. We're almost there."

Just breathe for Daddy.

His reassuring words soothed her, and she did as he said and took several deep breaths.

Just breathe for Daddy.

Daddy. He was her Daddy. Kade was *her* Daddy. Could life get any weirder? Was he only wanting to be her Daddy because she was in trouble? She hoped not because it would break her if he decided he didn't want her. He squeezed her hand again, and all those fears disappeared from her mind, replaced with the fear of the situation they were currently in.

"I'm scared," she said in a small voice.

Her Little side was floating just below the surface, and she knew it was because she was afraid.

"I know, baby. I'll keep you safe, though. I'm not going to let anything happen to you. You trust me?"

She didn't even have to think about it before she nodded. "Yes. I do."

He squeezed her hand one more time before he pulled his away and put it on the steering wheel as he took another turn. They were only a block away from the entrance of the compound, and as they approached the gates, she saw the line of men she considered family standing with guns in their hands, ready to fight for her safety at a moment's notice.

The men parted just enough for Kade to pull into the parking lot and then immediately moved back together to block anyone else from getting into the compound as someone started sliding the gate closed. Instead of driving back to the clubhouse, Kade pulled into one of the open bays of his custom motorcycle shop. Someone immediately pulled the bay door down as Kade got out of the car.

"Stay here and do not get out of the car. If you get out before I come get you, I'm spanking your ass."

He shut the car door before she could respond, and she heard him barking orders at whoever was in the garage, and then suddenly there was a large biker standing next to her door, making it so she couldn't get out of the car if she tried.

The minutes that passed felt like hours as she waited for Kade to return. Who had followed them? And why did they want her? Tears streamed down her face, and she wished she had her teddy bear to hold for comfort.

When the passenger door finally opened, Kade leaned in and unbuckled her and then scooped her up in his arms. Letting out a soft whimper, she snuggled into his chest and let him carry her without fighting it.

"I got you, baby," he murmured as he carried her into the clubhouse, walking directly back to his apartment.

She fell apart in his arms as soon as he closed the door behind them. Kade sat down on the couch, setting her on his lap as she cried into his shirt. He rubbed her back and whispered reassuring words to her until her eyelids felt so heavy, she just couldn't keep them open any longer.

When she woke, she was still on Kade's lap, and she knew she'd slept for a while. When she shifted, he looked down at her and gave her a soft smile.

"Hey, sleepy girl. Sleep well?"

Sighing contentedly, she stared up at him and nodded. "Better than I have in a long time with the exception of last night."

The next question that came out of his mouth she hadn't been expecting.

"When's the last time you had a Little day?"

Her eyes widened, and she wasn't sure if she wanted to answer that, but she also knew Kade would know if she were lying to him. He seemed to be able to sense that kind of stuff. "I'm usually Little whenever I'm at home. When I leave the house, that's when people see my dark side."

Slowly nodding, he seemed to think about that before he spoke again. "Well, you're at your temporary home, and we aren't leaving anytime soon so how about you spend the day in Little Space. It will be good for you to get your mind off stuff."

Hmm. He had a point. Then a question of her own popped into her head. "When's the last time you Daddied someone?"

His deep green eyes studied her and it almost seemed as though the flecks of gold in his irises were sparkling.

"It's been a while and it was at a club."

She let out a deep exhale. Was that relief she was feeling that it had been so long for him? "Why don't you spend the day in Daddy Space with me? I've never been Little around a Daddy. I've always wondered what it would be like."

ELEVEN
KADE

She was asking him to Daddy her. How could he say no to that? Fuck. He couldn't. He'd wanted to Daddy her ever since she'd turned twenty-one. The night of her birthday, he'd so badly wanted to spank her ass for having so many drinks and that's when he realized he wanted to be her Daddy.

"You know if I Daddy you, you'll have to be a good girl and obey the rules, or you'll get into trouble?"

Her pupils dilated and she shifted her body, squeezing her thighs together, making his cock thicken in his jeans.

"Yes," she whispered.

He wanted to see her Little side, and he wanted to flex his Daddy side too. He may have declared that she was his, but once he went into that space with her, there would be no turning back. She would be his forever.

"We need to sit down and go over rules, limits, and safewords first."

He noticed her nipples pebble under the thin T-shirt she was wearing. His baby girl liked the idea of rules. If she'd never been Little around a Daddy before, she'd probably never experienced having boundaries. It would be interesting to see if she was a rule follower or if she would be naughty. He had a feeling she might be a bit naughty.

She nodded. "'Kay."

"Did you bring any Little stuff with you? Clothes, toys, blankets?"

Shaking her head, she ran her finger over the bear patch on his cut. "No. Only my teddy bear and Binks."

Hmm, he didn't like that she didn't have her normal stuff that she had around her when she was in Little Space. He could grab some supplies from the closet that all the club Daddies kept stocked for situations like this. Even though it wouldn't be *her* stuff, it was all new, and it would get them by until he felt it was safe enough to go back to her apartment.

"How old is your Little side?"

She pulled her lip between her teeth. "I'm not sure. I think kind of young."

Okay, that was good to know. She was a small Little. He liked that. It meant more control, and he liked to be in control. "What do you like to do while you're Little?"

"I like to draw and color. And watch movies. I have some dolls too that I like to play with. They're princess dolls."

Smiling, he nodded. "Princess dolls for a princess."

"Why do you call me princess?"

He hadn't expected that question, but it made him smile. "Because when I walked in your bedroom, my first thought was, this is a princess's bedroom."

She grinned and nodded. "I like princesses. But I like the villains too."

"You can like both," he said as he reached out and brushed a wild piece of hair away from her face. "Do you have any limits I should know about? Limits around discipline or things you don't want to experience as a Little?"

"I just don't want to be treated badly. Like, I've read some forums where some Littles get treated horribly by their Daddies and I don't like that."

Furrowing his eyebrows, he cupped her chin. "I would never treat you badly. I'll spank your bottom when you're naughty or I might put you in timeout or have you write lines, but I would never be mean to you or treat you badly."

"I know. I know you wouldn't ever do anything like that. But you asked so I wanted to be honest."

She was so sweet and innocent. Even though they weren't fully in their headspaces, he knew her Little was right at the surface, and he liked seeing this side of her.

"Thank you for being honest. If you were ever scared or felt like I was doing something you didn't like or you just needed things to stop, you would always have a safeword. Do you know what a safeword is?"

"Yes. I've never had one but I've always thought about what it would be if I did."

He smiled. "Did you come up with one?"

Nodding her head, a shy smile spread across her face. "Pickle."

Holding his hand up to his mouth, he tried to hold back his laugh, but he just couldn't do it. "Why pickle, baby?"

Scrunching her face up, she made an ick face. "Because have you ever tasted a pickle? Yuck."

It took him a second to get his shit together and stop laughing, but when he did, he nodded. "Okay, baby. Pickle it is. You're allowed to say it anytime you need things to stop, even if we're in the middle of a discipline session."

She squirmed at the mention of discipline. He'd also noticed it the first time he'd brought it up. She liked the idea of being disciplined. He liked the idea, too, and his painfully erect cock really liked it. He was pretty sure her creamy white skin would turn the most beautiful shade of red under his palm.

"Let's talk about rules. Do you have any rules for yourself when you're in Little Space?"

She shrugged her shoulders. "Not really. I'm a princess; I've always done what I want."

He could see the defiance in her face. "Well, that's going to stop now, Princess."

TWELVE
REMI

Why was all this talk about rules and punishment making her feel so squirmy? She'd never actually been disciplined, but it had always been a fantasy.

"These are the rules I will set for you for now. First, always be honest and tell me if something's bothering you or if you're not feeling well or anything. Open communication is important to me. Second, be respectful to Daddy because I will always be respectful to you. Third, I will take your safety very seriously so no texting and driving, always wearing your seatbelt, eating regularly, no climbing on chairs or counters to reach for stuff, holding the railing when going up and down the stairs, no talking to strangers."

She giggled. "I have to talk to strangers when I'm at work."

"Yes, but when you're at work, you're in a big headspace and you're in a controlled environment."

"Okay."

He seemed pleased with that answer. "Good. I'll probably think of some rules as we go but those are the most important ones for now. Any questions?"

"Do you want me to call you Daddy?" She could feel his

cock pressing against her bottom and she was glad she wasn't the only one having a reaction to all of this. Being this turned on was completely foreign for her.

He stared at her for a long moment. "Do you want to call me Daddy?"

Slowly, she nodded her head, keeping her gaze on his. "Yes," she whispered.

Kade swallowed and gave her a sharp nod. "I'd like that too."

Suddenly, his lips were on hers as he wrapped one arm around her lower back. His cock dug into her ass as he deepened the kiss with his tongue. Wrapping her arms around his shoulders, she kissed him back, whimpering into his mouth as he nipped at her bottom lip.

Kade's hand slid up her back and into her hair, closing it into a fist at the base so he could control her movements. She wasn't very experienced with kissing so she liked that he took over and took what he wanted while still making it good for her.

When he finally pulled back, they were both panting as they stared at each other. Her lips felt swollen and raw but she wanted more. Moving her hips against his cock, she moaned but he moved a hand to one of her hips, stilling her.

"Be patient, Little girl."

She stuck her bottom lip out in a pout. "Meanie."

He threw his head back and laughed, then pushed her back farther onto the couch. "I know. Such a big ol' meanie. Better get used to this mean Daddy because I'm not going anywhere."

Good, because she didn't want him to go anywhere. She'd fantasized about this man for so many years, it still didn't feel real that she was in his apartment at the compound, talking about rules and limits for their dynamic. Life could be so wild sometimes.

He stood with her in his arms and set her down on the couch. "I'll be back in a few minutes. Stay here."

When he came back with several bags in his hand, she eyed them, nibbling on her bottom lip. "What's all that?"

Raising his eyebrows, he sat down next to her with a smirk on his face. "Things so you can enjoy your time being Little."

Kade opened one of the bags and pulled out several items, all of them toys. Coloring books, dolls, Barbies, a tea set. As he handed her each toy, she got more and more excited. She loved the dolls. They were so perfect. Even though they weren't her dolls, they would still be fun to play with.

"Oh, this one is so pretty!" she cried out when he handed her a lifelike baby doll.

He smiled at her and watched as she held the doll in her arms and rocked it. It was odd because she didn't feel shy or embarrassed expressing her Little side to him, and he looked so pleased that she was excited. Maybe it should have felt weird, but it was Kade. It felt natural.

As she continued to rock the doll, he started pulling out more items. A sippy cup, a pacifier, a soft blanket, clothes. So many pretty things that had her oohing and aahing. When he held up a pink frilly dress with lace underneath the skirt that made it flare out, she squealed and set the baby down.

"This is the prettiest dress I've ever seen! I've never seen anything like this."

"That's because it's custom. I have a friend in Seattle, and his Little girl owns a custom online Little shop, and she makes all the clothes herself. We ordered a bunch from her to have at the clubhouse."

Looking up from the dress, she stared at him in surprise. "You keep all this stuff at the clubhouse? I thought maybe Steele let you borrow some stuff."

"Nope. All of this stuff is yours now. All the Daddies in the club have a shared closet that we keep stocked with things in case any of us ever need it for a Little."

Her heart fluttered in her chest. She'd always adored all the men in the MC but knowing that they did something so simple but thoughtful made her love them all even more. "I love it. Can I put it on?"

"Let's finish looking through everything and then we can get you changed."

She felt her cheeks heat at the idea of him helping her change. How would she keep her wet panties a secret if he helped her?

Ignoring that thought, she reached out and touched the sippy cup. It was clear pink plastic. She'd always wondered what it would be like to drink out of one. Kade must have noticed her intrigue because he took the cup from her hands and went into the kitchen. He spent several minutes washing it in the sink before he opened the fridge and pulled out a jug of juice. She watched as he filled the cup and screwed the lid on tightly before bringing it over to her. When she reached for it with one hand, he didn't release it to her.

"Two hands."

Lifting her other hand, she wrapped both of them around the cup and then studied it before she slowly brought the spout to her lips. She glanced at him, but he just nodded and smiled, so she took a pull from the cup and immediately felt herself sink deeper into Little Space, feeling smaller than she'd ever felt before.

He sat down next to her again, and when she lowered the cup from her mouth, he reached out and swiped his thumb over her bottom lip where a drop of juice landed. Then he held his thumb in front of her. "Open."

She quickly obeyed, and when he slid his finger between her lips, she closed them around him and sucked the juice from his skin, their eyes locked on each other. Letting out a low growl, he pulled it free from her mouth and raked his hand through his hair. "Good girl."

Warmth spread through her body. She was a good girl. *His* good girl.

"Come here," he said, holding his hand out for her after she set the sippy cup on the end table.

She stood from the couch and moved in front of him, trembling slightly. Even though she was standing and he was sitting, he was still eye level with her. He reached out and started unbuttoning her jeans, and she hoped he wouldn't notice how wet her panties were.

He tugged her jeans down her legs. "Hold onto my shoulders and step out."

Obeying, she put her hands on his muscular shoulders, holding back the moan she was feeling as his hands brushed against her skin. He was so buff, and she wanted to spend hours tracing the lines of his tattoos all over his body… preferably with her tongue.

Don't think about that now. Your panties are already wet enough.

Focusing on anything but her dirty thoughts, she looked around the small apartment. Every member of the club had their own apartment with a tiny living room, a kitchenette, a bedroom, and a bathroom. Some members lived at the compound full time, and some had their own houses outside of the compound but would stay in their apartment at various times depending on what was going on with the club.

"Arms up, Princess."

Looking at Kade, she realized he was about to take off her shirt, leaving her standing in front of him in just her bra and panties. When he looked at her expectantly, she quickly lifted her arms in the air. A shiver ran through her entire body when he lifted the shirt off.

"Cold?"

She nodded, though that wasn't the entire reason for her shiver. He shot her a look that told her he knew she was bullshitting, but he didn't say anything. When he reached behind her and unsnapped her bra, she panicked and brought her hands up to her boobs to keep the material over the small mounds.

"Arms down. Don't hide from me."

Biting her bottom lip, she kept her arms in place. "My boobs are small and disappointing."

Kade reached out and cupped her chin so she was forced to focus on him. "Nothing about you is disappointing, Remi. I've seen almost every bit of you when you've worn those skimpy-ass swimsuits that made me want to spank your ass for showing off what was mine. You're perfect, and I promise you, your boobs are fucking beautiful."

Her eyes widened as he used his free hand to adjust his visibly hard cock. He'd watched her? She'd be lying if she said she hadn't worn those swimsuits in hopes to get him to notice her. She was secretly doing a fist pump in her mind at the knowledge that it had worked.

"Arms down. Don't make me start counting, Princess."

Slowly, she lowered her arms to her sides, letting the thin material of her bra fall down her arms. Kade licked his lips as he stared at her rosy buds for several seconds before clearing his throat and lowering the dress over her head.

"You really wanted to spank me for wearing those swimsuits?"

He helped her find the armholes and then nodded. "Hell, yeah. I hated that other men were seeing your body. I'm a selfish bastard, Remi, and I don't share. If it were up to me, you'd have been in a one-piece swimsuit that covered your entire bottom and breasts."

She was so used to men at her job hitting on her whenever she wore scantier clothes. It did something to her that the man in front of her wanted to keep her covered up so only he could see her body.

"It's up to you now," she whispered.

Her pussy pulsed as she said it. She was giving him control of her body and her life. The idea of that made her nipples ache with need. She'd never understood why she'd always gotten so turned on with the idea of someone controlling her, but she did, and she'd finally gotten to the point that she wasn't going to keep questioning it because for whatever reason, it's what she wanted and needed, and there was no other person in the world she wanted to give that control to.

Nodding, he smiled at her. "It is up to me now, and the only person that will see you in those skimpy-ass bikinis from now on is your Daddy. We'll get you some cute bathing suits with frilly shit on them for when you're around other people."

"Okay."

"Good girl. Hold onto my shoulders again and step into these bloomer panties."

She looked down to see him holding a pair of bloomers that matched the dress he'd just put on her. Smiling, she grabbed hold of his shoulders and lifted one foot at a time, stepping into them. When he pulled them up her legs and settled them on her hips, his hands brushed against her bottom, making her suck in a breath.

Lowering his hands from her body, he grabbed one of the dolls and held it out for her. "Time to play, Little girl."

THIRTEEN
KADE

It was still so strange to see Remi in pink, but she looked adorable in the frilly dress that barely covered her bottom.

He could hardly wait to put her hair in pigtails, but one thing at a time.

"What do you want to do first, Princess?"

She looked around the room at all the toys he'd brought in and then focused on the dolls and pointed. "I want to play with the baby dolls."

He nodded. "Go for it."

Pulling out his phone, he sent a quick text to Bear to see if he'd throw together some kind of meal for them for lunch. They'd missed breakfast and he was feeling like a crappy Daddy already. Bear responded almost immediately and told him he would bring some food over in a few minutes.

The next text he sent was to Steele to ask him what he'd told all the guys about why Kade had brought Remi to the compound. After sending the text, he focused his attention on the adorable Little girl in front of him, delicately brushing out the doll's hair. She glanced up at him shyly. Was she nervous to play in front of him? She shouldn't be, but she also mentioned she'd never been Little around a Daddy. Which pleased him way more than it probably should have. The possessive side of him was thrilled that she hadn't been with any other Daddies. He wanted to be her one and only.

The Daddies that belonged to the MC were all open about being Daddies, so it wasn't like she hadn't been around plenty of them over the years. But he guessed that since everything was so new that she was hesitant to really show her Little side. It would come in time. He couldn't rush her. He would just have to show her that she was safe to be herself with him and slowly encourage her Little to come out.

A knock at the door made her jump and look up at him with wide, worried eyes.

"It's okay, Princess. It's just Bear bringing food."

She relaxed a little but stayed completely still as he walked over to the door and opened it, taking the tray of food from his friend and then closing the door again.

He walked over to her and sat down on the couch, setting the tray on the small coffee table. "Come sit here so I can feed you," he said, pointing between his legs.

Getting to her feet, she took the few steps over to him and sank down between his legs facing him, making him realize that was a horrible idea. His cock pressed painfully against the zipper of his jeans. When he looked down at her, he inwardly groaned. She was staring up at him with those dark, round eyes that melted him.

Reaching for the tray, he picked up the peanut butter and jelly sandwich that Bear had used a bear-shaped cookie cutter to cut and held it up to her mouth. "Take a bite, baby."

Opening her mouth, she kept her gaze on his as she took a bite. As she chewed, he took a bite of the sandwich and then held it up to her mouth again. "You know you're safe to be Little and play in front of me, right?"

"I'm just nervous. I've never played in front of anyone except Carlee. It's usually just been me when I've been Little."

He motioned for her to take another bite. "Why have you kept your Little side a secret?"

She shrugged and swallowed the mouthful of sandwich. "I don't know. I think I was afraid that because I have a certain style that people would think I was faking being Little."

"I'm sorry you were scared to share that side of you. For the record, I want to spank your ass for not telling me years ago."

Giggling, she shook her head. "You never asked."

Shooting her a look, he held a piece of watermelon up to her mouth. "Brat."

As she ate the sweet melon, she did a little wiggle of contentment, making him smile.

When she finished her bite, her eyebrows pulled together. "Everybody is going to know I'm Little now, huh?"

"Not if you don't want them to."

This time she shot him a look. "Everyone knows you're a Daddy. If they know we're together, they're going to know I'm Little."

He shrugged. "Does it bother you if people find out?"

She thought about it for several seconds before she finally shook her head. "No. I guess not. I just... what if they think I'm weird?"

Hooking a finger under her chin, he stared down at her. "If anyone treats you badly because you're Little or says anything that makes you feel like they aren't being nice, you tell me and I'll kick their ass."

Letting out a sigh, she nodded. "Thank you, Daddy."

He beamed at her calling him Daddy. It was so damn sweet. "Say it again."

"Say what again?" she asked.

"Say what you just said again."

The look of confusion on her face was adorable, and then she must have realized what he was wanting because her cheeks turned pink.

"Thank you, Daddy," she said in a small voice.

Damn. Just damn. He felt as though he'd won the lottery. Leaning down, he brushed his lips over hers gently. "You're welcome, Princess."

He finished feeding her the sandwich and fruit and when they were done, he helped her to her feet. "Let's go potty and then you can go back to playing with your dollies."

Her cheeks turned pink. "I don't need to go."

Tilting his head, he raised an eyebrow. "Are you sure?"

She thought about it for a second and then furrowed her eyebrows. "How did you know?"

Chuckling, he took her by the hand and led her to the small bathroom. "Daddies just know this kind of stuff. Want my help?"

Letting out a squeak, she shook her head. "I can do it. I'm a big girl."

"Are you sure? Because you look like a Little girl to me. A super cute, Little princess girl."

Her eyes sparkled, but she shook her head. "I can do it by myself, Daddy. I need to goooo."

Grinning, he left the bathroom, pulling the door almost closed behind him. He pulled his phone from his pocket and opened his messages to see what Steele replied.

> Steele: As of right now, everyone except Rock knows that Remi is in trouble and that she's here for protection. They've all sworn to keep it quiet so Rock doesn't find out.

> Steele: Ivy is bugging me for a play date, though. I don't know how long I can keep her from forcing her way into your apartment to play with Remi.

Kade chuckled and shook his head. Ivy was a handful but seeing as Carlee hadn't been around much lately, Ivy was the perfect Little for Remi to play with. Hopefully, the two would hit it off.

The bathroom door opened, and he slid his phone back into his pocket, giving her all of his attention. She shuffled over to where she'd left her dolls and looked down at them hopefully.

"Play, baby. Get comfy and have fun. Want Daddy to turn on a movie for you?"

Clapping her hands together, she nodded. "Yes, please! Can we watch *Sleeping Beauty*? Her dress is so pretty!"

"Not as pretty as your dress."

Her cheeks turned bright pink as she twisted her hips to make the skirt flare out, making her giggle. He grinned and used the remote to find the movie she wanted to watch while she settled onto the floor with the dolls. When the movie started, he leaned back on the couch, but the only thing he was interested in watching was the sweet Little girl who was stealing his heart.

FOURTEEN
REMI

By dinnertime, she was feeling so much better. Spending time in Little Space was definitely the best way to forget about the real world and live in a land of make believe for a while.

Kade left his apartment for a few minutes to grab some food for them. Normally, whenever the MC guys stayed in their apartments at the compound, they would eat dinner in the gathering area with the rest of the club members, but since her dad lived there and ate with everyone every night, she and Kade couldn't exactly just prance out there without a million questions.

She was still in her pretty pink dress, but all her toys were set aside and she was curled up on the couch drawing with colored pencils while watching an animated movie. Kade had watched three movies with her and he'd even brushed one of her dollies' hair. He didn't do a very good job of it, but she wouldn't tell him that. She just thought it was so sweet that he had joined in on her day.

Surprisingly, he hadn't really bossed her around or gotten all strict Daddy on her all day. It was a little disappointing. Not that she wanted him to be bossy and strict all the time, but she'd never experienced that at all, so she was kind of looking forward to it. Her body was looking forward to it too, based on the reactions she had every time she thought about Kade getting all stern with her.

When he returned with a tray of food, she smiled at him as he set it down on the coffee table in front of her. Looking over at the pile of food, her tummy rumbled. Bear must have cooked dinner. He was the best cook out of all the guys and his meals were always mouthwatering.

"My princess is hungry."

My princess. Sheesh. He could be so swoony sometimes.

Reaching out to grab a plate, she startled when he lightly smacked the back of her hand. "Little girls don't feed themselves."

Biting her bottom lip, she hoped he didn't see her heart practically beating out of her chest and her nipples budding against her dress. Thankfully, the material was thick, so when she glanced down to check, it wasn't obvious.

She watched as he cut up a piece of chicken into small bites before spearing a piece onto a fork. Pressing the piece of meat to his lips, he quickly blew on it before moving it to her mouth and waiting until she opened her lips so he could feed her. Letting out a moan, she closed her eyes and hummed happily. Yeah, Bear was definitely the best cook ever.

When she opened her eyes, Kade was staring at her with so much intensity in those green irises of his that she looked around nervously. "What?"

Shaking his head, he cleared his throat. "You're the most beautiful, sexy woman I've ever laid eyes on, and when you moan like that, it makes me want to do filthy, depraved things to you just so I can hear those noises some more."

Food no longer appealed to her. She was still hungry but not for what was on the plate. "Can we skip to that?"

Narrowing his eyes, he shook his head. "Don't tempt me, Little girl. You need to eat dinner."

Well, maybe she wanted to tempt him. Leaning over, she brought her face close to his and stuck out her bottom lip in a pout. "Please, Daddy. I've been such a good girl today."

She could tell he was struggling to keep his composure but then suddenly he cupped her chin and tilted his head, his lips turning up into a smirk. "Are you trying to top me from the bottom, Little girl?"

Crap. He was on to her. Sucking in her lip, she widened her eyes and gave him her best innocent look. "I would never do that."

He snorted and shook his head. "You're going to find yourself with a red bottom if you keep it up. Open."

Sighing, she opened her mouth and accepted the bite he offered. Well, that just sucked. Having sex with Kade would seriously be the best thing ever. The thought of losing her virginity to the man she'd been crushing on for years made her pussy ache with need.

He continued to feed her for several minutes until she rubbed her full tummy and shook her head.

"Come on, Princess. It's bath time."

Say what? Bath time? Like as in he was going to take a bath with her or he was going to give her a bath? Either way he would see her naked, and he would know how turned on she was. Well, it wasn't like she couldn't see his arousal. She could see that enormous thing pressing against the front of his jeans. Surely it wasn't that big once he removed his pants and underwear, right?

Taking her hand, he led her into the small but clean bathroom and pointed toward the toilet. "Go potty."

Hesitating, she looked at the toilet and then back at him, but he was busying himself with getting the bathwater running and pouring bubbles into it. "Bubbles!"

Turning to look at her, he nodded. "Yep, but you can't get in until you go potty, so you better get it done."

Lowering her eyes, she lifted the toilet lid and reached

under her dress to pull down the matching bloomers and her panties. Since the water was running, he wouldn't hear her pee, so maybe she could do it with him in the same room. Thankfully, he didn't pay any attention to what she was doing, so she was able to quickly pee and clean herself up before she stood and flushed the toilet. Going to the sink, she washed her hands while watching him in the mirror as he tossed several toys into the water and set a washcloth on the edge of the tub.

Turning around, she stood shyly, unsure of what she was supposed to do, but luckily, Kade didn't make her wait. He walked over and knelt in front of her before reaching up under her dress and pulling down the clothing she'd just pulled up. As soon as the cool air touched her pussy, she shivered.

He rose and stared at her as he reached down and pulled her dress up over her head, leaving her standing in front of him completely naked. When she raised her arms to cover her hard nipples, he caught her wrists and shook his head. "Little girls aren't allowed to hide from their Daddies."

Shuddering, she nodded. Would she ever get used to him referring to himself as Daddy? It was still so strange when he called her Little girl, but at the same time, it felt so natural too. Maybe because she'd fantasized about him calling her that at least a million times throughout the years.

Without warning, he hooked his hands under her armpits and lifted her, then turned, setting her into the hot water. He didn't remove his hold until she was settled on her bottom. Apparently it was a bath just for her, which was perfect because she loved bath time and having him there, taking care of everything made it easy to slip right back into her smaller headspace.

Fishing through the water, she found one of the toys he'd dropped in and grabbed it. She inspected it and grinned. It was a mermaid doll that had a moving fin if you wound it up and then set it in the water. She had pink hair and was the most beautiful mermaid ever.

Kade knelt beside the tub and grabbed the washcloth he'd set out, dipping it into the water before squirting a large amount of what looked like some kind of body wash made for kids onto it. She held her breath as he reached out and started running the cloth over her shoulders. It smelled like bubblegum.

"Breathe, Princess. Daddy is just taking care of you. Your only job is to focus on playing with your toys."

Glancing up at him, she found that he looked genuine, so she went back to fishing out the other toys to find out what they were. Getting lost in play, she didn't really pay attention to him as he lifted one arm and washed it, then the other. Her attention quickly moved to him when he ran the washcloth over her nipples, sending a zing to her pussy.

He gently washed one of her breasts, seeming to linger just briefly on her nipple before he moved to the other one and washed it. When he moved down her tummy, she felt herself holding her breath again as his hand traveled lower and lower until it was between her legs.

"Spread your legs so I can wash your pussy, baby."

Hesitating, she looked up at him. "I can do it."

Shaking his head, he pinned her with a stern look. "Daddy is doing it. Spread your legs, Princess."

Slowly, she widened her thighs and whimpered as his hand brushed against her clit. It wouldn't take much to have an orgasm. After all, she'd pretty much been on edge ever since he'd shown up at her apartment the day before. When he circled her clit, she grabbed hold of the side of the bathtub and moaned. "Daddy," she murmured.

He smiled and continued washing her folds. "Such a needy Little girl."

Before she could respond, he moved the cloth away from her pussy and started washing her legs, both a relief and a frustration.

"Play with your toys, Princess."

She wanted to play, but not with her toys, but she didn't say that. Instead she grabbed her mermaids and went back to playing until she was lifted out of the water and set on the bathmat outside the tub. He wrapped her up in a thick towel and then picked her up and carried her into the bedroom to set her down on the edge of his bed. Just like the bathroom and living room, the bedroom was clean and cozy and smelled like leather and musk, just like Kade.

As he started drying her off, she felt herself blushing. He was taking care of her in such a sweet and intimate way that she would have never expected out of Kade. He'd always been so gruff and growly, but this was such a different side of him. She suspected it was a side that not many people ever got to see.

"When was your last relationship?" she asked.

She didn't really know why she'd asked it or what she wanted his answer to be, but she wanted to know.

Kade eyed her as he ran the towel over her skin. "It's been a little over four years."

Looking at him in surprise, she thought about that in her head. He hadn't had a relationship since she was twenty. And he'd told her he'd noticed her on her twenty-first birthday. Had he not had a relationship because of her? "You haven't had sex in four years?"

He shrugged. "Once. It was a casual hookup at a club in Seattle."

"That's surprising," she murmured.

He lowered a soft nightgown over her head and helped her find the armholes. "Why's that?"

"I don't know. You're hot. I've seen the way women look at you. And I thought men had needs."

Kneeling in front of her, he held a pair of cotton panties that had princess crowns printed all over them by her feet. They were adorable.

"I took care of my own needs. I don't really know about the

way women look at me because I've only been looking at one woman for the past couple of years."

Holy moly, macaroni. Was he talking about her? She was pretty sure he was, but she still couldn't believe he'd liked her for that long. As he pulled the cotton panties up her legs, he looked up at her, his eyes burning into her soul. Swallowing thickly, she slowly nodded.

Grabbing hold of her hands, he pulled her to stand so he could settle the panties over her bottom, his large hands running over her cheeks, making her shiver.

"When's the last time *you* were in a relationship?" he asked.

Shaking her head, she watched as he rose, towering over her. "I've never been in one."

His eyebrows drew together in confusion. "What do you mean never? You've had boyfriends, haven't you?"

It was embarrassing to admit, but she'd been so busy having a crush on him all these years that she'd never gone out with anyone. "No. I've never had a boyfriend."

"Have you ever been with a man at all, Remi?"

She could see him panicking, and she didn't know why. In all the books she'd read, guys always loved virgins. "No."

Taking a couple of steps back, he ran his fingers through his hair as he stared at her like she had three heads. "You're a virgin?"

Nodding, she lowered her gaze from his, feeling so immature and stupid, but instantly, Kade was in front of her, cupping her chin so she was forced to look up at him.

"Fuck," he murmured, letting her chin go. "Fuck. Remi. Shit. You're a virgin, and here I am corrupting the shit out of you. Baby… shit. Fuck."

Why was he freaking out? He looked like he was in full-blown panic mode as he started pacing in front of her. "I'm sorry," she whispered.

He froze mid-step and looked at her. "Why are you sorry?

You don't need to be sorry. I need to be on my fucking knees begging for your forgiveness. I had no idea you hadn't been with a man, and I've been rushing you into this with me. Your dad is going to hate me if he finds out."

Taking a deep breath, she walked over to him and stopped only a few inches away. She was so small compared to him that she barely even came up to his chest so she always had to crane her neck to look up at him. "Kade, my dad loves you. He would probably be thrilled if I ended up with you instead of some guy he doesn't know. And you're not rushing me. I want this. I've always wanted this. That's why I've waited..." She trailed off.

"Why have you waited?"

Fidgeting with the hem of her nightgown, she forced herself to keep her gaze on his. "Because I've wanted you since I was a teenager, and no other guy ever even compared to you. I wanted you to take my virginity."

Suddenly she was swept into his arms and was on her back on the bed with him hovering on top of her, their lips centimeters apart. The scent of his cologne surrounded her and she could feel his erection digging into her thigh.

"Remi, if I take you, virgin or not, there's no out. It's you and me forever. I've wanted you for years, and once I have all of you, I'm never letting you go. I'm not going to fuck you yet because I want you to think about if this... if I'm what you really want. If you really want me as your Daddy, controlling your entire fucking life. Because that's what it would be, Princess. You'd be my Little girl, and I'd be your Daddy, and there would never be another woman in my life, and there damn sure wouldn't be any men in your life besides me. Understand?"

She knew he said all that to try to scare her away, but all it did was turn her on even more, and she found herself wrapping her legs around his waist, lifting her hips against his cock. "I want you, Kade. I want you to be my Daddy. Forever. I know this," she motioned to the two of them, "is new but I've known you all my life, and I know your heart, and you're everything I've ever wanted out of a man and a Daddy."

He stared down at her for a long moment before his lips crashed onto hers, kissing her deeply and thoroughly. When he pulled away, she whined in protest.

"You still need to think about it, Remi. I'm not fucking you until you're sure."

Shooting him an exasperated look, she sighed. "I am sure, Kade."

"No. I need you to be sure, sure. I need you to be in love with me before I take your virginity. That's a special gift that I'm not just going to take from you."

Dropping her head back onto the mattress, she let out a long dramatic sigh. "Had I known you would be this stubborn about it, I wouldn't have told you."

Raising his eyebrows, he brought his hand down on the back of her thigh with a loud smack. "If you hadn't told me, I'd be blistering your ass when I found out. You don't keep things from me. Got it?"

And that was one of the reasons she cared for him so much. Reaching down, she rubbed the back of her thigh but he quickly caught hold of her wrist and raised it over her head, pinning it to the bed. "No rubbing. You need to feel that as you fall asleep. I need to go meet with the guys, and you need to go ni-night."

Sticking out her bottom lip, she pouted. "You're not gonna stay with me?"

He brushed his lips over hers. "I won't be long. I need to update everyone on what's going on so we make sure we're keeping the compound and all the women safe. As soon as I'm done, I'll come snuggle you."

"Can I have Binks and my teddy?"

Smiling, he nodded. "Of course you can. Crawl up under the covers and I'll get them for you."

He released her and she hesitantly crawled up to the head of the bed and slid under the soft covers, waiting for him to bring her toys. When he returned to the bedroom, he had both stuffies and something else in his hand.

Reaching for the toys, she hugged them to her chest as soon as he released them to her and when she opened her eyes, he was holding a pink pacifier up to her mouth.

"I thought you might want this for bedtime."

She studied the device. It was larger than a normal pacifier but it was so cute, and she'd always wanted to try one, so she reached up to take it, but he pulled his hand away. When she dropped her hand, he held it up to her mouth again, waiting for her to open. Slowly, she parted her lips, and he slid the soft nipple in.

"Good girl. I'll be back soon. I'm taking a baby monitor with me and the other part is right on the dresser so if you need anything, just call out for me."

Nodding, she felt her eyes getting heavier by the second as she suckled on the binky. Who knew it could be so soothing?

Kade leaned down and kissed her forehead. "Night, Princess."

Before he even left the room, she was already tumbling into a deep, comforting sleep.

FIFTEEN
KADE

He needed air. It felt as though he couldn't breathe. She was a virgin. And not only was she a virgin, but she hadn't had sex or been in a relationship because she'd wanted him for so long.

Carrying the baby monitor, he shut his apartment door and walked out to the community room where he found Steele sitting on the couch with Ivy curled up on his lap watching a movie. Bear was on the other end of the couch drinking a beer. Storm and Talon were shooting a game of pool. Doc and Faust were standing at the bar watching. Rock and Silver were nowhere to be seen. It wasn't unusual for Rock to not be there, he was an early-to-bed kind of guy, but Kade had no clue where Silver was. The guy seemed to be acting strange lately and not staying at the clubhouse very often anymore. Maybe it was simply because his relationship with Carlee was new and he was spending a lot of time with her.

"Need a meeting," Kade said as he walked through the common area to the meeting room that had a long, scratched-up wooden table in the middle of it with chairs surrounding it.

Everyone stood and followed him.

Steele set Ivy on the couch where he'd been sitting and

tucked blankets around her. "I'll be back soon. Come get me if you need anything."

Ivy nodded and popped her thumb into her mouth as she went back to watching the movie. It was adorable, and Kade looked forward to getting the two women together for a Littles play date.

When everyone was in the room, Kade began to close the doors, sending Ivy a wink when she looked over at him as he closed her off.

Before he could say anything, the room erupted in questions.

"Is Remi okay?" Bear asked.

Talon crossed his arms over his massive chest. "Who the fuck is after her?"

"Is she yours?" Doc asked.

Storm was scowling. "Who the fuck do we need to kill?"

Looking at everyone, he shook his head and the room finally went quiet as they waited for him to answer all of their questions. "She's mine. Any of you make any kind of move on her and I'll kill you."

All the men grinned and shook their heads. Steele chuckled. "Told you when you found your Little, you'd be just as possessive as me."

Giving Steele the bird, Kade grinned at his friend. He hated it when the fucker was right.

"We don't know who's after her. Did anyone get the plate numbers on the truck that followed us?"

Talon shook his head. "There was mud rubbed over the plates so we couldn't see anything. The only thing we could see through the tinted windows was one person driving, but we couldn't make out anything else."

Great. Just fucking great. They had nothing to go on.

"We need to keep the compound security tight. Right now, it seems like the person is just stalking Remi, but her ties to the club are known in Shadowridge, so we don't know for sure they aren't targeting her because of us. That means all the old ladies need to have someone posted on them at all times when they aren't here at the compound," Kade told them.

Everyone nodded their agreement.

"I'm going to assign some prospects to watch her apartment for the next few days to see if anyone shows up there, but my guess is if they were following us here, they know she's not at home."

Doc nodded. "Whatever you need to keep her safe, you know we have your back."

He smiled at his friend and then at the rest of the men who were all nodding. Pulling his eyebrows together, he narrowed his eyes. "Where the fuck is Silver?"

Steele shrugged, looking just as irritated as Kade felt. "Haven't heard from him all day. Has Remi talked to Carlee recently?"

Kade shrugged. "I think so, but I'll ask her. I need to get back to her, but I just wanted to let you guys know what's going on."

Storm walked over and slapped Kade on the back. "We're here for you, brother. You know how we all feel about keeping women and Littles safe."

"Thanks. You guys are my family. You're her family too."

Talon nodded. "Damn right. She's like a niece to me."

Shooting his friend a look, Kade grinned. "That's all she better be to you."

The room erupted in shouts and laughter as some of the men called him a possessive asshole. He grinned and nodded as he flipped off the room and walked out toward his apartment. He loved those bastards in there. Even if they were all assholes sometimes.

When he walked into his apartment, it was quiet and dark except for the bathroom light, which he'd left on for her so she wouldn't be scared. He moved as quietly as he could, stripping out of his clothes down to his underwear before he slid into bed next to her. As soon as he was settled, she scooted over until her body was plastered against his, but he could tell by her breathing she was still asleep. It was going to be a long, painful night for his cock, but he wouldn't have it any other way.

Wrapping an arm around her, he kissed the back of her head and closed his eyes.

Waking up with Remi curled up in his arms was what he imagined when he imagined heaven. She was so soft and fit perfectly against his body. He knew he was already in love with her. Maybe he had been for years, but spending the last couple of days with her sealed it in cement. She was a virgin, though, and more than a decade younger than him, so he needed to give her the time and space to decide if he was what she truly wanted.

Stroking his thumb over her bicep, he watched her sleep for over an hour before her eyes fluttered open and she stretched, which caused her ass to rub up against his hard cock. He was blaming morning wood for it, but he knew it was all Remi causing the hardness.

With a soft hum, she rolled back slightly and looked up at him. "Morning."

Leaning down, he brushed his lips against hers. "Morning, Princess."

"I didn't even hear you come back in last night."

Smiling down at her, he nodded. "You were fast asleep. Maybe the pacifier helped you get some rest."

She looked around on the bed and then grabbed the pacifier that must have dropped out of her mouth at some point in the night. "I always wanted to try one because they seemed so soothing. I liked it more than I expected."

Nodding, he took the device from her hand and set it on the nightstand. "Good. We'll make sure you have one for naptime and bedtime."

Biting her lower lip, her gaze lowered and she shifted her hips back against his cock. Groaning, he put a hand down on her to still her movements before he embarrassed himself. He was going to need an ice-cold shower. "Quit teasing Daddy," he growled into her ear.

She let out a long, deep sigh. "But I wanna play."

"How often do you play with your pussy, Princess?"

Her cheeks turned rosy. "Every day usually."

Okay, he hadn't been expecting that answer. So she was a virgin but she wasn't completely inexperienced. It made him happy that she'd explored her body and pleasured herself. Not that she would ever have to pleasure herself again because that was his job now. "And you haven't gotten to play in a couple of days. I bet you need to come, don't you?"

Nodding, she raised her dark eyes to his. "Yes."

Moving his hand from her hip, he tugged her nightgown up and ran his hand up her tummy, feeling goosebumps rising on her skin along the way. She uttered a small moan as his hand moved over one of her breasts, cupping it. Using his index finger, he circled her nipple several times until she was squirming against him.

Switching to the other breast, he gave it the same treatment, and the tiny moans and whimpers that escaped her lips were nearly enough to make him explode, but he forced himself to ignore his own needs so he could focus solely on making her feel good. He wouldn't fuck her, but that didn't mean he couldn't make her come other ways.

"Daddy," she whimpered.

Leaning down so his mouth was near her ear, he let out a

low growl. "You're going to be a good girl for Daddy and obey my every command."

Bobbing her head up and down, she moaned. "Yes. I will. I'll be a good girl."

Smiling against the shell of her ear, he nipped at it. "You better be, otherwise Daddy will punish you and you won't get to come."

She cried out and nodded. "Yes, Daddy."

Fuck, he was going to die of arousal. Rising up onto his forearm, he shifted so he was hovering over her. Reaching between them, he grabbed the hem of her nightgown and yanked it up over her breasts, immediately lowering his head to her dark pink nipple to suck on it. As soon as he latched on, she arched her chest up higher. Closing his hand over the other breast, he gently tugged on it while licking and sucking on its twin until she was begging.

"Please, Daddy. Please, please, please," she whimpered.

He kissed his way down her tummy, and when he got to her panties, he peeled them off her hips and down her legs, leaving her pussy fully exposed to him. She was completely bare already, but he could hardly wait to shave it for her going forward.

Hooking his arms under her thighs, he lifted them, setting them over his shoulders before he dipped his head down and gave her pussy a long lick along her lips. "Has anyone ever licked this pussy before, Princess?"

Just because she hadn't actually had sex didn't mean she hadn't ever fooled around with anyone, but she quickly shook her head. "No. No one has ever touched me."

Holy fuck. He would probably go to hell for the possessiveness he was feeling over her, but he couldn't help it. She was all his.

Lowering his face, he licked again, using his thumbs to spread her open for him as he started sucking on her clit. Her head fell back against the mattress as she cried out, her legs jerking against him. Swirling his tongue around the delicate pearl, he groaned. She tasted like honey. So damn sweet and irresistible. She was also soaked.

As he continued to lick and suck, he brought his index finger to her opening and slowly nudged it in. She was so damn tight around just his one finger that he knew he would hurt her the first time he put his cock in her, and he hated that knowledge. He never wanted to hurt his girl, so he would have to do whatever he could to make sure she was completely ready when the time came.

As he inched into her, she cried out, and the walls of her pussy pulsed around him as he did. When he was to the second knuckle, he curled his finger upward, making her scream out. Sucking hard on her clit, he did it again and again until her entire body was shaking while she screamed out her orgasm.

It was several minutes before she quieted and went limp. Chuckling, he gently licked her pussy clean, savoring every last bit of flavor before he lifted her legs and lowered them onto the bed so he could move up next to her. As soon as he was beside her, she rolled into him and buried her face in his chest, and everything was absolutely perfect in the world. At least it was while they were in their own little bubble together.

SIXTEEN
REMI

Holy crap.

She'd had orgasms before. Hundreds of them. She loved orgasms. But her orgasms had never in a million years felt like *that*. That was beyond anything she could have ever thought it could feel like. The man knew what he was doing, that was for sure.

Too relaxed to move, she cuddled into him and sighed contentedly while he stroked her back and whispered soft words to her. She was too floaty to hear everything he was saying, but she heard the words good girl being used repeatedly and that was good enough for her.

At one point, she must've fallen asleep because when she opened her eyes, Kade was no longer on the bed, and she could hear the shower running. The need to pee was strong, and if she waited any longer, she would probably end up wetting the bed. Deciding she better hustle, she went to the bathroom and was going to knock but realized he'd left the door partially ajar.

"Daddy," she called out.

"Come in, Princess."

Pushing the door open, she smiled when she saw him

looking at her through the glass shower. Slowly, without meaning to, her gaze traveled down, down, down and holy shit. That thing was a monster. His deep chuckle brought her back to reality, and she looked up at him with wide eyes.

"Did you need something, baby girl?" he asked with a smirk.

Suddenly remembering her bladder, she quickly nodded. "I need to go potty."

Nodding, he pointed toward the toilet. "Go ahead. Do you need Daddy's help?"

Letting out a small squeak, she quickly shook her head. "No, thank you."

Rushing over to the toilet, she was relieved that it was on the other side of the shower, but then she realized he could still see her if he looked in the mirror on the wall across from them. Luckily, he didn't seem to pay her any mind, but she couldn't seem to keep her eyes off the mirror as he used a washcloth to wash his naked body.

She did her business as quickly as she could and washed her hands before turning toward the shower to watch him even closer. It was probably rude to stare, but she couldn't seem to look away. Not that he seemed to mind based on the grin he was sporting.

"Something interesting there, Princess?"

"Uh huh," she murmured.

"Come get in the shower with Daddy. I'll wash your hair."

Swallowing, she pulled her nightgown up and over her head without hesitation before taking a step toward the shower. Kade opened the glass door for her to step in, and as soon as he closed the door behind her, he pulled her into his body. Splaying her fingers over his chest, she looked up at him as he lowered his face to hers and kissed her. It was so light and gentle at first, but it turned more and more intense with each passing second. Slipping her hand down his front, she wrapped her fingers around his thick shaft, making him groan into her mouth.

He pulled back and stared down at her, bringing his hand down to hers to still it. "No touching."

"Please, Kade? You made me feel so good and I want to try to make you feel good too."

"Daddy."

Furrowing her brows, she looked up at him with confusion. "What?"

"My name is Daddy."

Sheesh. Why was that so damn hot? She had no freaking clue, but it made her pussy ache with need.

"Daddy, please?"

He groaned and released her hand. "You don't have to."

"I know, but I really want to. I might be bad at it, though."

Shooting her an exasperated look, he shook his head. "There's no way you could be bad at it, baby. Just having your hands on me is pure heaven."

Biting her lower lip, she looked down at his cock in her hand. Her fingers didn't even connect because of how thick he was. "Can you tell me what to do?"

As he rolled his head back, his jaw tensed, and when he looked down at her again, his eyes were blazing. "Fuck, you're so perfect for me. Keep your hand just like that and slide it up and down my cock."

Doing as he said, she ran her hand up and over the velvety tip and then back down again, repeating it several times. Kade let out a low groan as he raised his hand to the back of her head, taking a fistful of her hair into his palm.

"I'm not going to last long, Princess. I've been riding the edge for the past few days."

She smiled at that thought because she'd been feeling the same way. "Can I taste it?"

His eyes widened slightly as he stared down at her. "You want to taste my cock?"

Nodding, she continued moving her hand up and down his shaft, loving every second of it and the way it seemed to affect him. "I want to suck on it."

He cursed under his breath and finally nodded. "You can suck on it, baby, but I'm only gonna last a few seconds between those beautiful lips."

It was amazing how powerful she felt, knowing that he was so close to coming because of her and what she wanted to do to him. Reaching out, she placed a hand on his stomach for balance as she lowered herself to her knees. When she let go of his cock, it bobbed in front of her face until he wrapped his hand around the base.

"Only take in as much as you can handle. If you don't want to swallow it, take your mouth off my cock when I tell you I'm going to come."

Oh, no, she was going to swallow every last drop because she could hardly wait to taste him. Opening her mouth, she stuck her tongue out and swirled it around the tip before wrapping her lips around the head. Kade groaned, which only spurred her on to take more of him until the tip hit the back of her throat, making her gag slightly.

Raising her eyes to him, she pulled back and sucked down again, going a little bit deeper before she gagged. His head was bent forward, watching her with a look of both pleasure and pain on his face. At first she thought she was doing it wrong.

"Fuck, baby, I can't hold back much longer," he ground out.

Clamping her mouth around him tighter, she forced herself to relax her throat and suck him in even deeper. His hand found her hair and grabbed onto a fistful as she started sucking harder and faster.

"I'm going to come, baby."

She went deep and felt his hot come shooting into the back of her throat as he grunted and thrust into her mouth one last time before he stilled. Licking every drop off his cock, she hummed her approval at his flavor.

When he pulled back and out of her mouth, he reached down and gently helped her up to her feet before pulling her into his body and hugging her tightly.

Cuddling into his chest, she sighed happily. He held her there for several minutes before he moved her so she was directly under the shower spray. "Tilt your head back and close your eyes, Princess."

Doing as he said, she let him wash her hair, moaning softly as he massaged the shampoo onto her scalp. After her hair was washed, conditioned, and rinsed, he grabbed a washcloth and body wash. She let him wash her, feeling like a true princess as he massaged her muscles while he worked. When his hand went between her legs, she whimpered. She was still feeling sensitive from her mind-bending orgasm.

When he was done helping her rinse, he turned off the shower and grabbed a towel, wrapping it around her before grabbing a second towel for himself. Even though she'd known Kade for so long, it still shocked her how sweet and polite he was, always tending to her needs before his own. Not that she thought he was selfish or anything, because she knew he'd give his shirt off his back to anyone who needed it, but she just hadn't expected such gentle, caring treatment from him.

As soon as she stepped out onto the bathmat, he scooped her up and carried her into the bedroom before setting her on the edge of the bed. He left her there and went into the bathroom again, returning a few seconds later with her hairbrush and another towel. Smiling at him, she reached for the brush, but one sharp look from him had her dropping her hand to her lap. She sighed contentedly as he dried and then brushed her hair while she sat there like a good girl.

Everything was so strange. It was like they were in their own little bubble, and because of that, she was almost able to forget about the reason she was even at his apartment in the first place. She wanted to forget it all and focus on the budding relationship between them. To be able to explore her Little side and experience his Daddy side. But the reality of it was she was being threatened, and though she knew she was safe at the compound, she couldn't stay there forever.

"What did the guys say last night?" she asked reluctantly.

Kade continued to brush her hair. "Steele sent Rock out of town for a few days so you don't have to hide in the apartment the entire time you're here. We have a prospect sitting by your apartment at all times to see if anyone shows up."

Having her dad gone would make things easier. Not that she minded being cooped up with Kade. She could be Little when they were alone.

"Did you find out who was in that truck?"

He shook his head. "The plates were covered in mud and the windows were tinted."

She sighed and dropped her shoulders. Reaching down, she rubbed her tummy. It felt like it was full of rocks.

"What's wrong, Princess? Are you hungry?"

Shaking her head, she looked up at him worriedly. "No. My tummy is just upset. It feels like I'm just hanging in limbo waiting for the hammer to drop at any time, and I have no idea who the hammer is. What if they're actually dangerous? Obviously they have no boundaries if they went to all that trouble to take photos of me."

He reached down and gently cupped her chin, stroking his thumb over her jaw. "I wish I could make it all better for you, baby. All I can do is tell you that I will protect you with my life and so will the rest of the MC. You're safe with us."

Nodding, she forced a smile. "I know I'm safe with you. I need to go to work, though. You have to work too."

It was obvious he didn't like that, but he finally nodded. "Yeah. I guess you're right. But I'm going to have some guys at the bar with you whenever you're at work if I can't be there."

Her eyes widened. "Daddy, you can't just come stand post at my job."

Raising an eyebrow, Kade tilted his head. "Either I have someone at your job or you don't go to work. You choose. You're not leaving this compound without an escort."

The stubborn side of her wanted to argue and tell him she could do whatever she wanted, but her stubborn side was nowhere to be found because she was practically turning to goo right before him over his overprotectiveness.

"Okay," she murmured.

"Good. Let's get you dressed and go eat breakfast."

He held up a pair of pink leggings with a matching pink sweater. She shook her head. "I need black clothes."

"Don't you want to be Little today?"

Of course she did, but she couldn't go out of his apartment in all pink. "If we're going out there in front of people, I can't be Little."

"Why not? Almost all the guys out there are Daddies. Ivy runs around here in Little Space almost all the time."

He was right about that, but no one in the MC had ever seen her in anything but black, and they might judge her. "They might think I'm weird for wearing pink or that I'm Little and never told them."

"Look at me," he demanded. "No one is going to judge you. We don't do that here. Honestly, I think they'll love seeing this side of you. And I know Ivy would love to have some play time with you."

She would enjoy having a friend to play with. It had been way too long since she and Carlee had a Little Space play date. She really needed to text her friend and try to schedule a girls' day.

Her Daddy was right about them not judging her. Deep down, she really did know that but it was still scary.

"Trust me, Princess?"

How could she possibly say no to that? She couldn't, so she nodded. "Okay, Daddy."

Smiling at her, he leaned down and kissed her forehead. "My brave girl."

As he dressed her in a pair of pink panties, leggings, and sweater, she was in pink heaven. It was all so cute and comfortable. She protested when he lowered the sweater over her head without putting a bra on her, but he told her she was too Little to wear a bra. When she started to protest again, he gave her a stern look that quickly had her closing her mouth.

When she was dressed, he pulled her hair into a ponytail on top of her head and added a pink bow to the base. Looking at herself in the mirror, she automatically felt so Little. "Can I bring Binks?"

"Of course. Come on." He offered his hand and led her from the apartment.

Having Binks in her arms helped her anxiety as they made their way to the community space. As soon as they walked in, several men looked up from what they were doing. She stepped closer to Kade, hiding behind him slightly.

Storm walked up behind them and gave her ponytail a light tug. "Hey, Remi girl. You look adorable."

He winked at her and continued walking toward the kitchen. Storm was… well, he was just like his name. If you were in his circle, you were safe, but anyone who messed with him or his circle… they got to experience the Storm.

Kade pointed toward the large dining table where Faust and Gabriel were eating breakfast. "Go sit down and I'll bring you your breakfast."

Looking up at him with pleading eyes, she shook her head. "I wanna stay with you."

When had she become so needy?

He squeezed her hand and nodded. "Okay, baby. Come on."

Doc passed them as they made their way to the kitchen,

and to her relief, he didn't say anything. Instead, he just smiled indulgently at her and then nodded toward Kade.

When they walked into the kitchen, Bear was there, pouring pancake batter onto a griddle. "Morning." He glanced at Remi and offered a smile. "Morning, Remi."

Bear looked intimidating, but he really was just a big teddy bear on the inside. She'd always loved the man. He was incredibly sweet to all the women and Littles. "Morning, Bear."

"Give me five minutes and I'll bring you out some pancakes," Bear told them.

Nodding, Kade went over to the coffeepot and poured a cup of coffee before opening a cupboard full of sippy cups, taking a moment to choose one. He filled the cup with milk and twisted on the lid before grabbing his cup of coffee.

"Come on, Princess."

After following him out to the dining table, she stood awkwardly, unsure of what to say to the two men who glanced their way. Luckily, the awkwardness didn't last because Faust pulled out the chair next to him and patted the seat. "Sit down, Remi."

She glanced up at Kade and he nodded, so she sat down and smiled shyly. "Thanks."

Her cup was set in front of her before her Daddy lowered himself into the seat next to her.

"Morning," Kade said to the men.

Gabriel smiled at them but didn't have a chance to respond before they heard an excited squeal as Ivy came skipping toward them.

"Remi!"

Grinning at Ivy, she waved, and suddenly, having a Little friend there with her at the breakfast table made things not feel so scary anymore.

SEVENTEEN
KADE

The women chatted enthusiastically with each other until Bear brought out a stack of pancakes and set them in the middle of the table. Then he set a pink plastic plate directly in front of Remi that had a pancake in the shape of a bear's face, complete with blueberry eyes and a whipped cream smile.

She looked up at Bear with a wide grin. "Thanks, Bear."

"Welcome, sweetheart. I'll bring you one too, Ivy," he said before disappearing into the kitchen again.

Ivy clapped her hands. "One of the best things about being Little is when Bear makes fun foods for me."

Steele shook his head, but he had a smile on his face as he stared adoringly at his Little girl. "You're one spoiled Little girl."

When Kade looked down at Remi, she was already digging into her pancakes and somehow had whipped cream on her hands. Grabbing a napkin, he reached over and cleaned her up, winking at her when she looked up at him. It seemed all the nervousness she'd been feeling before they'd left the apartment was gone, and she was in full Little Space. He hoped to keep her in that headspace all day to keep her mind off things.

He was still reeling from his orgasm in the shower. Having her mouth on him was heaven, and watching as she sucked him down made it impossible to hold off. It had been everything he could do not to carry her out to the bedroom and fuck her right then and there. She needed time to figure out if she was sure, though. He also didn't just want to take her impulsively. It was important that her first time was special and that he took extra care to make it as comfortable as possible for her.

He felt a tug on his cut and when he glanced down, he realized Remi was already done with her breakfast.

"Can we go play in the playroom?" she asked quietly.

Glancing over at Ivy who was also done with her breakfast, he nodded. "As long as Steele is okay with it too."

The girls squealed and scrambled to get out of their seats, joining hands as soon as they were close to each other while making their way into the playroom that was set up for Littles. It was full of books and toys and comfy seating so Daddies could sit in there with their Littles if they wanted to.

As soon as they were out of sight, Kade realized he already missed her. Steele and Gabriel chuckled, making him look over at the two men. "What?"

Steele had a shit-eating grin on his face. "You're in love."

Shrugging, he tried to brush it off, but his friend was right. He was head over heels in love, and he just hoped Remi would feel the same way about him some day.

Gabriel nodded toward the playroom. "She's adorable, though. She's always been adorable even in all black, but it's cool to see this side of her too."

Smiling at his friend, Kade was grateful for the chaplain. Gabriel was one of those people you could tell anything to and he would never tell a soul. They'd had a few heart-to-hearts over the years and he was the only one in the club who knew he'd had feelings for Remi for years. "Thanks, man."

The men sat around the table and talked, and soon, other men joined them: Talon and then Bear and then Storm. Silver was nowhere to be seen, which for some reason was starting to get under Kade's skin. There was something about the guy he just couldn't put his finger on.

"So what's the plan?" Faust asked.

Kade sighed. "She's going back to work tomorrow. I need at least one or two men on her at all times when she's at work. She's not happy about it, but she doesn't get a choice in the matter of her safety."

Faust grunted. "Good."

Grinning at the grumpy man, Kade nodded. "I'm behind on some jobs, so I'm going to go back to work tomorrow too. I'll have some prospects accompany her to work and stay posted there during her shift. So far, the person leaving the letters has only left them at her apartment. I doubt anyone would be ballsy enough to do anything at The Hangout where a bunch of bikers are always hanging out."

Steele nodded, seeming to be deep in thought. "She hasn't had anyone at work hitting on her or acting strange?"

Shaking his head, Kade shrugged. "Not that she can think of. She said she has people hitting on her all the time, but that's pretty normal when you work in a bar."

Talon snorted. "Rest in peace to whoever you ever see hit on her when you're there."

Yeah. He was right about that. The thought of other guys hitting on her or possibly even touching her made his blood turn cold. He needed to talk to her about her job and find out if she was working there because she wanted to or if it was just a money thing. Because if she was only working there for money, she could quit tomorrow, and he could take care of both of them. He wasn't rich by any means, but he had a healthy savings account, and his business was consistently getting busier every day.

His phone vibrated with a text message from one of the prospects.

> Ink: We've seen a black pickup truck driving past her apartment a few times. The plates are still covered but we noticed there's red paint on the left side back bumper.

"Fuck," he murmured.

All the men looked at him with confused expressions.

Letting out a sigh, he read them the message.

"Fuck. Well, at least we have something to help identify the truck." Steele muttered.

Kade shook his head as he reread the message. "Steele, can you reach out to the sheriff and ask for him and his guys to keep an eye out for a truck with mud over its plates? That alone is enough to pull them over."

"Of course. You sure you want to let her go to work tomorrow?" Steele asked.

Shrugging, he sighed. "We can't hide here forever, and she won't go anywhere without security. So far this person hasn't tried to hurt her physically. We just need to find whoever it is and stop it from continuing."

Everyone nodded, then they heard a loud thump from the playroom and suddenly everyone was on their feet running toward the sound. When Steele and Kade made it to the doorway first, they found both girls on the floor with several books surrounding them like they'd been dropped from above.

"What is going on here?" Steele demanded.

Ivy instantly looked guilty while Remi looked at Kade nervously.

"We were trying to reach some books on the top shelf," Remi admitted quietly.

Looking at the bookcases, Kade shifted his attention to the top shelf, which was at least three feet taller than the women. "How exactly were you trying to reach them?"

Both women were on their feet now, and Kade noticed Ivy sliding her hands behind her bottom as she shifted from foot to foot.

Steele pointed at her. "Little girl, did you two try to climb up the bookshelves?"

Remi glanced over at Ivy and then back at Kade, her bottom lip pulled between her teeth.

"No, we were trying to boost each other up on our shoulders so we could reach," Ivy admitted.

As he narrowed his eyes at Remi, she lowered her gaze from his and started fidgeting with the hem of her shirt.

The other men had already left the scene, leaving only Kade and Steele staring into the room at the Little girls.

"Have we not visited this subject before about reaching for the books that are higher? Because I'm pretty sure you spent some time over my lap the last time you did it," Steele said firmly.

Ivy glanced over at Remi and then down at her feet. "Sorry, Daddy."

Nodding, Steele stepped back. "Not as sorry as you're going to be. Our apartment. Now."

Shuffling forward, Ivy left the room with Steele right behind her, leaving Kade staring at his own naughty Little girl.

Crooking a finger at her, he pointed at the floor in front of him. "Come here."

Her eyes widened, but she shuffled forward until she was only inches away from him.

"Do you think climbing on each other's shoulders was a safe thing to do, Princess?"

Dropping her shoulders, she shook her head. "No. I didn't think we would fall, though."

Reaching out, he cupped her chin. "It doesn't matter if you thought you would fall or not. Safety is a very serious rule, and climbing on top of each other was not safe. If you wanted the books off the top shelf, all you had to do was ask. There is a whole clubhouse full of tall men that could have easily reached them for you. Right?"

She nodded, her eyes wide with worry. "Sorry, Daddy. I won't do it again."

"I know you won't. But you're still going to get a spanking to help remind you not to do it again. Let's go to our apartment."

Taking her by the hand, he started leading her out of the room but she stopped suddenly. "Can I get Binks?"

The stuffed bat was on the floor near all the fallen books, so he released her hand and nodded. "Go ahead."

She quickly grabbed the bat, hugging it to her chest as she took his hand again and followed him toward the apartment.

As soon as they were inside, he turned to her. "Go put Binks on the bed, and then you need to go stand in the corner for a few minutes to think about how what you two did was dangerous and how you both could have been seriously hurt."

After a brief hesitation, she turned and went to the bedroom with him following close behind. She tossed Binks on the bed and then looked back at Kade. "You're gonna watch me while I'm in the corner?"

Nodding, he crossed his arms over his chest. "Yep. Now, pants and panties off before you go."

Her eyes widened. "Why do I have to take them off?"

Walking over to her, he pinned her with a stern look. "Because naughty Little girls have to have their bottom on display while they're serving time in the corner."

Without waiting for her response, he hooked his thumbs in her leggings and panties and pulled them down her legs. Since she was still barefoot, he didn't have to remove her shoes before she put her hands on his shoulders and stepped out of her bottoms.

Rising, he pointed toward the corner. "Go on. Ten minutes."

Her mouth dropped open but she didn't argue. Instead, she turned around and shuffled to the corner at a snail's pace.

"Time doesn't start until you're actually in the corner," he told her.

"Well, that just sucks," she murmured.

"Excuse me, Princess?"

"Nothing, Daddy."

Uh-huh. Nothing, his ass.

EIGHTEEN
REMI

Had he forgotten to set the timer? Because it felt like she'd been standing in that stupid corner for at least an hour. And the entire time she stood there, all she could think about was her upcoming spanking, which, based on her no-pants situation, she guessed would be on her bare bottom.

She was having mixed feelings about it. Filled with trepidation for sure, but also kind of excited to experience her first spanking. It couldn't be that bad, right? It was just some swats on the bottom. Except Kade had enormous hands, and she wasn't sure how light his swats would be.

When the timer on his phone finally went off, she startled and turned to look at him. He raised an eyebrow at her and crooked his finger for her to go to him. The look on his face made her tummy do several flips. She had a feeling it wasn't just going to be some swats. Was it too late to try to get out of it?

"When we talked about safety rules, didn't we talk about not climbing on stuff?"

"Well, yes, but you said no climbing on chairs or the counters. I didn't climb on either of those."

Maybe that would help. Maybe he would realize that she hadn't known that climbing on Ivy's shoulders would be against the rules. The look on his face told her he wasn't buying any of it.

"Little girl, don't try to get out of this with a technicality. Climbing on someone is the same thing as climbing on chairs or counters. When you two decided to climb on each other, did you not think it was dangerous and you could possibly fall?"

Well, crap. She really wanted to lie, but she had a feeling he would know, and then she'd be in even more trouble. So instead, she nodded. "I knew one of us could fall."

He nodded and grabbed hold of her wrist before pulling her over his lap in one swift move. "Breaking the rules, especially health or safety rules will always get you put in this position. Your safeword is pickle, and you can use it if you need to."

Without warning, his hand landed on her bottom, and she let out a loud yelp of surprise, but before she could do anything else, his hand was already coming down with rapid force on her cheeks.

"Ouchie!"

Smack! Smack!

Wiggling on his lap, she tried to break free, to get away from his punishing hand but he had such a firm hold on her that she wasn't able to move at all, so she tried another method. She started kicking her feet as she cried out, apologizing for her transgression. The only thing that accomplished was Kade throwing one of his thick legs over both of hers, pinning her in place under his hold.

"Daddy, I's sorry! I won't do it again."

He paused. "You better not do it again, otherwise next time, you'll experience a lot more than just my hand on your bottom."

She was relieved that he'd stopped spanking. That hadn't been so horrible. Definitely bearable. Though she wasn't so sure she'd actually learned any kind of lesson. "I won't, I promise."

"Good."

Smack! Smack!

She cried out in surprise as the spanking started up again, this time harder and faster than before. He peppered her entire bottom all the way down to the tops of her sensitive thighs, which really hurt. Emotions started to bubble up, and it didn't take long before tears started falling from her eyes.

"I'm sorry, Daddy! I's so sorry!"

He ignored her pleas and continued to punish her bottom. It was painful and caused her to cry, but it wasn't so unbearable that she wanted to say her safeword. It actually kind of felt good to let out the emotions that had been building up over the past few weeks. Suddenly she let out a sob and then another one until she was crying hysterically over his lap as tears poured out of her. Giving in to the spanking, she went limp and let it all out.

The spanking stopped as quickly as it started, and she was shifted up so she was sitting on his lap with his arms wrapped around her. She continued to sob loudly, unable to get herself under control, but Kade didn't seem to mind. He just held her and rocked her in his arms while stroking her back.

"Let it all out, Princess. Daddy's got you. Just let it all out. I know it's been building. I got you, baby."

His reassuring words calmed her. She was a messy crier, and she knew it but she felt safe letting herself go with Kade. Thank goodness she didn't have her usual makeup on because that would have been a mess. Letting her tears continue to fall, she buried her face in his chest and melted into him, and when the crying finally subsided, she felt completely drained but also completely refreshed. It felt as though everything that had been running through her mind for the past several weeks was gone and she felt peaceful.

Kade shifted, and she realized he'd stood up with her in his arms and carried her to the bed before setting her down. "Crawl into your spot, baby. Let's rest for a while and I'll hold you."

Wincing as she tried to scoot on her bottom, she rolled over onto her hands and knees and crawled up to the side she'd slept on the night before. Her tender bottom was definitely on display for Kade as she went, but she couldn't find it in herself to care. She just wanted to get to the snuggling part because somehow being in his arms made everything feel not so scary.

She watched as he pulled his shirt up and over his head and kicked off his boots, leaving him in his jeans as he climbed into bed next to her. Before she realized what he was doing, her pacifier was brought to her lips, and she opened her mouth to let him slide it in. As she suckled on the soft nipple, she felt so Little and cared for. Who would have thought getting her bottom spanked would have made her feel cared for? But it did.

Wrapping an arm around her, he pulled her into his chest and stroked her back until her eyes felt too heavy to keep them open any longer.

"Baby girl, you need to wake up."

"Mmm, no, thank you."

Kade chuckled. "Yes, baby. You're not going to be able to sleep tonight if you don't wake up. It's already after lunch."

Letting out a dramatic sigh, she groaned and opened her eyes to find him propped up on his forearm, staring down at her. His blond hair hung around his face, and she couldn't resist reaching up to touch it.

"How are you feeling?"

How was she feeling? Rested. Light. Comfy. Aroused. So

many feelings. Shifting slightly, she winced. Oh, but her poor bottom was still sore.

Raising an eyebrow, he smirked at her. "Still sore, huh?"

She nodded. "Yeah. But other than that, I feel good. Lighter. I think I needed a good cry."

"I think so too. Sometimes Little girls need a good hard spanking to help them let it all out."

The memory of the spanking made her pussy ache. She'd felt so submissive and Little when she'd been over his lap and even though it had hurt, it had also turned her on and since she still didn't have panties on, she could feel her arousal between her legs.

Looking up at him, she stuck out her bottom lip slightly. "Can we have sex?"

His lips pulled back in a smile, but the look in his eye told her she wasn't about to get what she wanted.

"Nope. Little girls don't get pleasure after a punishment. And besides, we are waiting to have sex until you're ready."

She huffed and glared at him. "But I am ready. I want to be with you."

"You sure about that? Spankings and rules and over the top protectiveness? You sure you're truly ready for all that?"

He was asking like he thought she was going to back out, but she'd never been more sure of anything in her life. He was it for her, and she was madly in love with him. The spankings, the rules, all of it, she wanted and needed.

"Yes, Kade. I'm positive. I know what I want. I want this. I want us."

"I don't want broccoli."

Raising an eyebrow, Kade leaned over and put his mouth

next to her ear. "Well, you're going to eat the broccoli because it's good for you, or you'll be spending more time in the corner."

Dropping her shoulders, she glared at the pink plate in front of her. Broccoli was so gross. It was like trees that got wet and wilted and smelled like grass. Who would think, hey, I wanna eat that? Uh, no one, that's who.

Kade reached out, picked up a piece of the yucky green stuff from her plate, and held it up to her mouth. "Open."

Exchanging glances with Ivy, who was sitting across from her and had already gotten scolded for not wanting to eat her potatoes, Remi sighed and looked down at the bite he held in front of her. Yuck. But the only alternative was the corner and she definitely didn't want to spend more time there, so she slowly opened her mouth. As soon as he placed it in her mouth, she moaned as all the flavors hit her tongue. She had no idea what was on the little green wilted trees, but they tasted buttery and delicious.

"See. You never know until you try it," Kade scolded softly. "Besides, you force your dad to eat that stuff all the time so you should too."

Well, he had a point there. But her dad was recovering from a heart attack. So there was a difference.

Her Daddy continued to hand feed her the broccoli until it was all gone, and for some reason, when he fed her like that, it made it seem even yummier. Maybe it was because every once in a while, one of his fingers would dip inside her mouth and she would lick it. Kinda kinky but she found it hot.

The rest of dinner went without a hitch, and she was feeling less and less weird about being around all the guys while she was in her Little Space. None of them acted like she was weird or seemed to judge her. In fact, they seemed to be indulging her Little and being sort of Uncle-ish toward her. It was sweet. Even Faust, who was the grumpier one of the group, had reached out and used his napkin to wipe ranch dressing from her cheek.

"Come on, Princess. Let's go get you a bath and ready for bed. It's going to be a long day tomorrow."

She could tell he wasn't happy about her returning to work, and really, she wasn't thrilled about it either, but she had rent to pay and a car payment and she wasn't selling any of her sketches yet, so unfortunately, working at the bar was her only option for the time being. Her dream of being a sketch artist wasn't taking off as quickly as she'd hoped.

Waving goodnight to Ivy, she took Kade's hand and followed him to the apartment. Even though she'd had a nap earlier in the day, she was feeling sleepy and relaxed. It had been a really good day. She just wished Carlee had been there to enjoy it with her. The three of them would have had so much fun together.

He led her into the bathroom and pointed toward the toilet. "Go potty, Little girl."

It didn't feel as strange this time as she did her business while he got her bath ready. It was almost like they were falling into a routine, and she really liked that. She'd never liked the awkwardness of being around someone new, so it was really nice that she'd known Kade for so long, and it was as if they were able to skip that awkward phase altogether.

After cleaning herself up, she washed her hands and waited until he came over to undress her.

"Do you want your hair washed tonight?" he asked.

She shivered as he pulled her leggings and panties down. "No, thank you."

When she was completely naked, he found a hairband in the vanity drawer and wrapped her ponytail up into a bun, securing it with the band before he lifted her under her armpits and set her in the tub.

She squealed when she noticed the bubbles were pink. "I've never seen pink bubbles before."

"Every princess needs pink bubbles."

Looking up at him as he knelt beside the tub, she melted. This man was everything she'd wanted and nothing like she'd expected. He was even better than all her fantasies and expectations.

"Daddy?"

"Hmm?"

"Thank you… for everything. For helping me and being my Daddy and all of that. This has been the best few days of my life. I've never felt so cared for."

He studied her for several seconds. "Your dad has always loved and cared for you."

Nodding, she shrugged. "Yes, he always loved me and Atlas. We knew he loved us. But I think after my mom died, he lost part of himself with her, and while he did the best he could with us, he spent so many years grieving that sometimes, it felt like he wasn't there. He always cared for us but emotionally he was lost, I think. He's an amazing dad and I love him so much, but I think I lost out on that part, which I understand. I can't imagine losing the person I loved."

Cupping her chin, he offered a sad smile. "Your mom was an amazing woman and I know it was devastating for your dad to lose her. I know it was because of you and Atlas that he even survived through it all."

She nodded, thinking about her brother. Atlas had been the best brother ever, and she hated that he lived so far away. She could hardly wait to see him at Christmas time.

Kade started washing her, taking delicate care as if she was fragile. It was kind of silly seeing a big, tattooed biker kneeling at the side of the tub, washing her while she sat in a pool of pink bubbles. The thought made her giggle.

"What's so funny?" he asked.

Shrugging her shoulders, she gave him an innocent look. "Nothing, Daddy."

"Mmhmm. Brat."

She grinned as she played while he finished washing her body. As soon as he was done, he pulled the drain and lifted her from the water. Now that she was all clean, she wondered if she'd get to experience his mouth on her again before bedtime.

Unfortunately, that didn't happen. Instead, he helped her into some pajamas, then tucked her into bed, sliding the pacifier between her lips before he picked up a picture book and read it to her. Her eyes started getting heavy halfway through, and before the story was over, she faded to sleep.

NINETEEN
KADE

"If you feel like there is anyone in the bar giving you bad vibes, you signal to the guys and they will come right over."

Remi shot him an exasperated look. "Daddy, I know. You've told me this like twenty times. If anything makes me feel uncomfortable, even if I get a splinter, I'm to signal to the guys and they will come running."

It was his turn to shoot her an exasperated look. The little smart ass was halfway to getting her butt reddened before work. He was nervous about letting her go. He'd even considered not going to work and going to work with her, but she'd insisted that everything would be fine and she'd never felt threatened at The Hangout.

"Little girl, this is serious. We don't know who this asshole is, and we can't take any chances."

She walked over to him, lifting her hands to cup the sides of his face. He stared down into her dark eyes and his heart felt as though it was going to beat out of his chest.

"Daddy, I promise I'll be extra vigilant and the guys will be paying attention too. You don't have to worry. Everything is going to be fine."

"I do have to worry. You're my girl and I love you. If anything happened to you, I don't know what I'd do, Remi. I wouldn't fucking survive that."

Her eyes widened. "You love me?"

Shit. He hadn't meant for that to slip out but it had, so he just nodded. "Yes. I think I have for a long time, but I didn't realize it until the past couple of days."

Rising to her tiptoes, she pulled his face down to hers and kissed him. He wrapped his arms around her waist and lifted her so her feet were dangling in the air until she wrapped them around his waist and clung to him. Using his tongue to part her lips, he explored her mouth until they were both out of breath.

Her lips were swollen when he pulled away, but her eyes were sparkling as she stared at him. "I love you too, Daddy. So much."

"Really?"

Nodding, she grinned. "Yes. I don't want anyone else. I want you, and I want this. I want our dynamic, and I want to be your old lady."

Throwing his head back to laugh, he shook his head. "You don't get to be my old lady."

Her face fell, making him chuckle.

"You don't get to be my old lady because you're my Little girl."

She giggled and stuck her tongue out at him. "You're silly."

"I'm never letting you go, Remi."

"Good. Because I don't want you to."

Well, thank fuck for that because he would walk her down the aisle tomorrow if he could. Except there was the whole situation of her dad not even knowing yet. That was a slight problem, but one thing at a time. The more important thing at the moment was figuring out who the fuck was messing with his girl.

"Does this mean we get to have sex now?" she asked.

"Not right now, no. But maybe tonight. We'll see how you're feeling after work."

Letting out a long dramatic sigh, she rolled her eyes. "So mean."

Shaking his head, Kade set her on her feet and swatted her bottom, making her squeal. "I'll show you mean."

Raising his eyebrows, he started growling at her. She giggled and took off running with him right at her heels. He could have easily caught her. Her short little legs couldn't outrun him, but the chase was fun and she was giggling the entire time. When she got to the bedroom and jumped on the bed, he tackled her and started tickling her all over, making her scream out and cry for mercy.

"Wait! I'm gonna pee!"

He stopped the tickling and snatched her up from the bed to take her into the bathroom. Once they were there, he set her down in front of the toilet. "Go pee."

She was dressed in all black again for work, and even though they'd been playing around, she wasn't in her Little headspace, which he realized meant she wasn't quite as carefree about peeing in front of him. Crossing his arms in front of his chest, he waited.

"Kade, I need privacy," she murmured.

Raising an eyebrow, he stepped forward and clasped her chin between his fingers. "No privacy between us. Not when you're Little and not when you're big. And my name is Daddy. All the time. Understand?"

Her eyes sparkled, and he knew she liked it when he corrected her on his name. She liked calling him Daddy as much as he liked hearing her call him that.

"I need to go brief the guys that are going to work with you, so I'll give you privacy this once, but don't expect it again."

She nodded. "'Kay."

Maybe her Little was skimming the surface, which was just

fine with him. He liked seeing her teeter in between the two. Both sides of her were adorable.

Leaving the apartment, he went out to the community room where two more seasoned prospects stood waiting. "Don't fucking leave the bar. If you notice anyone flirting with her, I want photos of the person and a name if possible. Anything happens to her, it's on your head. Got me?"

Both men nodded. Kade liked them. They were close to making it into the club. But when it came to his Little girl, he didn't fuck around.

"If anything seems sketchy, you call me first and then call Storm and have him deploy people to The Hangout. And if something does seem sketchy, you get her secured somewhere where no one else can get to her."

Ink, the older of the two, nodded. "Don't worry, Kade. We will protect your girl with our lives."

After what he'd gone through with one of the last prospects who'd gotten kicked out of the club when Kade found out he'd been hitting his woman, he didn't think he'd ever trust anyone new to the club again. The prospect, Caspian, had tried to play the whole thing off as an accident, but they didn't buy his excuses. Abusing a woman was never an accident.

He trusted both Ink and Breaker, though. They were close to being voted into the club permanently, and both men deserved it. They'd shown their loyalty, and Kade already considered them his brothers. He'd still kick their asses if they let anything happen to Remi.

Nodding, he slapped the man on the shoulder. "Thanks, Ink. I'll check in with you guys throughout the day."

Remi appeared beside him with her backpack purse hanging over her shoulder. Even though he'd seen her in nothing but black for the past ten years, now that he'd seen her in pink for the last several days, it was kind of strange seeing her in black again. She looked just as beautiful, though, in her black, skin-tight ripped jeans, a black band tee, and black combat boots. She looked like a girl that could kick anyone's ass despite being so small.

Looking down at her, he pinned her with a stern look. "If Ink or Breaker give you an instruction, you follow it or you'll be one sorry Little girl. Understood?"

She glanced nervously at the prospects and then up at Kade before she nodded. He didn't want to be a dick, but he also needed her to understand that he wasn't fucking around when it came to her safety. If he had to paddle her ass to get her to obey when he or one of the guys gave her a safety order, he would do just that.

"Good girl. Keep your phone in your back pocket at all times and check in with me throughout the day. I'll check in with you and the guys too. Okay?"

"Okay, Daddy," she said so quietly that only he could hear.

Smiling at her, he wrapped his arm around her shoulders and pulled her into him, kissing the top of her head. "That's my good girl. I love you, Remi."

"I love you, too, Daddy."

TWENTY
REMI

As soon as Remi walked into The Hangout, she was busy with customers nonstop for the rest of her shift. Thankfully, most people who went there were regulars, so she could just look at them walking through the door and know what they wanted to drink.

Ink and Breaker sat at a table in a corner of the bar where they could see everything that was happening as well as who was coming and going. She did her best to ignore them and pretend they weren't even there, but when her boss, Tracy, walked up next to her while she was pouring a drink at the bar, she knew she was going to have to answer some questions.

"What's up with the bikers camping out at table nine?" she asked.

Remi got along with her boss, and Tracy always took the security of the team very seriously, so she really hoped the woman wouldn't give her any shit.

"Kade put them on me because of something that's going on."

Tracy looked her up and down while chewing her big wad

of bubblegum like she always did. "Kade, huh? You finally tie him down?"

Her eyes widened, making Tracy laugh.

"Don't think I didn't see the way you looked at him whenever he came in. You never looked at anyone else that way."

Feeling her cheeks heat, she nodded. "Yeah. We're together."

Nodding, her boss started to wander off. "Got it. You'll have a security detail with you from now on. Doesn't surprise me. Kade seems overprotective."

She giggled to herself. Overprotective was putting it lightly.

"Hey, Remi," a familiar voice said.

Smiling at her regular, she automatically started pouring him a beer. "Hey, Bill. How're things?"

The man sat down on one of the barstools and shrugged. "Hey, doll. Things are good. Same ol' stuff."

Sliding the beer across to him, she grinned. "Well, it's good to see ya."

"You'd be able to see me more if you said yes to letting me take you to dinner," he replied.

Shooting him an exasperated look, she rolled her eyes. "One of these days, you're going to find the perfect lady for you."

He shrugged again and took a drink from the frothy top. Bill had been a long-time customer at The Hangout and every time he'd come in, he'd always asked her on a date. She always said no, of course. The man was at least thirty years older, and khaki-and-plaid-wearing guys were definitely not her type. He also hung out at the bar nearly every day, which was kind of a turnoff. But he was nice enough, and whenever he was there, he would keep her company while she made drinks.

The rest of her shift went smoothly. Kade had sent her a text every hour asking if everything was going okay. She'd reassured him every time that everything was fine, though she wasn't surprised when he showed up with Steele and Storm about an hour before her shift was over.

He walked up and wrapped his arm around her waist, pulling her into his chest before he lowered his face to kiss her. "Hi, Princess."

Smiling up at him, she sighed. She didn't think she would ever get tired of looking at his handsome face. "Hi, Daddy. I missed you. Go sit with the guys and I'll bring you all a round."

Nodding, he released her and scanned the bar before leaving her to join the other men. When she went behind the bar, she started filling glasses with ice-cold beers.

"You and Kade, huh?" Bill asked.

The MC was well known at The Hangout. When they wanted to get away from the clubhouse for a drink, that was where they went. They'd also helped provide security over the years whenever there were live performances at the bar. To say the Shadowridge Guardians were loved in this town was an understatement. They were loved and respected by most. There were always a few people who judged them just by their looks, but she knew those were the kind of people who would judge anyone who was different than they were.

Smiling at the older man, she nodded. "Yeah."

Bill nodded and slid a twenty across the bar to her. "Have a good night, doll."

Taking the money, she called out her goodnight to him as she carried the tray to table nine where Kade and the rest of the men were sitting. She could feel Kade's eyes on her as she approached, and when she passed out all the drinks, he tugged on her hand.

"What were you and Bill talking about?" he asked.

"He just asked if you and I were together. He's such a nice guy."

Steele and Kade exchanged a look that had her pulling her eyebrows together. "What? Am I missing something?"

Shrugging, Kade pulled her onto his lap. "He's just a bit odd. He applied to be in the MC a year or so ago but he didn't even have a motorcycle. He said he would buy one if he could join because he'd always wanted to be in a motorcycle club. It was weird."

Hmm. Yeah, that was kind of strange. But she knew his wife had died a couple of years before, and maybe he was just hoping to find somewhere besides the bar to spend his time.

Shrugging it off, she stood from his lap and grabbed her tray from the table. "I need to get back to work. You hanging out here until I get off?"

He nodded. "You know it, baby. And I brought an extra helmet."

Grinning widely, she bounced on her toes. "You fixed your bike?"

"Yep, and I need my girl to break in the back seat."

It was so hard to contain her excitement for the next hour. Riding on the back of a Harley was one of her favorite things ever. The wind and vibrations as the bike sped through the city. Talk about mind-clearing.

As soon as the next shift of servers came in, Remi clocked out and grabbed her purse, meeting Kade by the front door where he waited for her. As soon as they were outside in the sun, she sighed happily while admiring his bike. She'd always loved the beauty of custom bikes. They were a work of art. She'd sketched many of them over the years.

Kade grabbed a full face helmet that was all black and shiny and she wondered if he'd gotten it just for her. It was just her style and when he slid it over her head, she was grinning at him before he flipped down the visor. She'd ridden on the back of enough motorcycles to know what to do and where to put her feet, so once he was on, she climbed on behind him and wrapped her arms around his waist, pressing her breasts into his back. She heard him let out a low growl before he started the engine.

The heavy vibration pulsing against her pussy while being plastered up against Kade was nearly enough to send her over the edge as he raced through the streets toward the compound. Steele led the group and Storm was beside them while the prospects were behind.

As they pulled into the compound, she felt herself grinning. She wished the ride had been longer but she'd take what she could get. Since she was actually dating a member of the MC, she was pretty sure she'd get the chance to ride behind him often.

Ivy was waving excitedly as they all lined up their bikes. Once parked, Kade helped her off the bike, and when she pulled off her helmet, he was on her, kissing her wildly. She was shocked at first but quickly started kissing him back, her nipples budding against his chest. When he pulled away, they were both panting.

"Whew, Daddy, I need a fan after seeing that," Ivy announced.

Steele plucked Ivy up into his arms and carried her toward the door. "You need to mind your manners, Little girl. Come on, Daddy's hungry."

Ivy giggled as he threw her over his shoulder. "I can make you a snack."

"I wasn't talking about food, Ivy," Steele replied as they disappeared inside.

Kade cupped Remi's face, resting his forehead against hers. "Still want Daddy to fuck your pretty little pussy?"

It felt like her heart was going to beat right out of her chest as she nodded. She wanted it more than anything.

He grabbed her hand and pulled her toward the entrance, and as they walked through the community room, he didn't stop to acknowledge anyone. Instead, he led her into his apartment, and as soon as the door was closed behind them, she was pushed up against the wall with his hand positioned loosely around her neck. They were both breathing hard as they stared at each other for a long moment before he used his other hand to grab a fistful of hair as he brought his mouth down to hers.

The mix of rough and gentle was overwhelming her senses and she was practically vibrating with arousal as he pressed his hips into hers. She could feel his erection through his jeans, and she wanted to get her mouth around it again, but he seemed to have other plans as he peeled her shirt up over her head, throwing it onto the floor.

Her nipples pressed against the thin fabric of her bra, and when he cupped one of her breasts and ran his thumb over the sensitive peak, her knees nearly gave out, but he was there, holding her up while he drove her wild at the same time.

"Are you sure you're ready for this, Remi?" His voice was gravelly and thick and only seemed to heighten her arousal.

"Yes. I want this, Kade. Please. Please, Daddy."

TWENTY-ONE
KADE

She was perfection. So soft and sweet while at the same time strong and brave. His girl. She was all his, and she wanted him. How lucky could one man get? Apparently pretty fucking lucky.

Reaching around her, he unsnapped her bra and pulled it away from her chest, leaving her completely topless before him. Smoothing his hand up her belly to her breasts, he cupped each one, giving each nipple a gentle tug before sliding his hand up to the base of her neck, squeezing the sides lightly.

"You're going to be a good girl and do what Daddy says, aren't you?"

Nodding, she stared up at him. "Yes. I'll be a good girl."

He smiled down at her before kneeling at her feet to remove her shoes and jeans. "Hold onto my shoulders and lift your foot."

As soon as she was standing before him completely naked, he leaned forward and pressed a kiss to her pussy, inhaling deeply to take in her scent. "We need to get you on birth control because I need to feel this pussy without any barriers."

"I'm on birth control already. I have been for years to regulate my periods."

Groaning, he kissed her pussy again. She was going to kill him.

"I got checked after the last time I was with someone. I'll show you the test results later and then we can talk about fucking without a condom," he told her.

Her fingers snaked through his hand, and when he looked up at her, she was staring down at him.

"I know you wouldn't lie to me. I don't want anything between us now."

If it was possible for his cock to get any harder, it did. He'd never fucked a woman without protection but the thought of anything being between them was unbearable.

Rising, he picked her up and carried her to the bed, setting her down gently before pulling his shirt up and over his head. As soon as he dropped it on the floor, her hands were roaming his chest, tracing the lines of his tattoos. When her hands lowered to his belt, he kicked off his boots and then helped her trembling hands to unbuckle and unbutton his jeans.

"Lie back, baby girl. I need to taste you."

Her pupils dilated as she scooted back on the bed and lowered herself to the mattress. Her creamy pale skin was such a contrast to the rosy color of her nipples and the pink coloring of her pussy lips. She was a work of art and yet she didn't have any ink on her entire body.

Pushing her legs apart as he crawled onto the bed, he felt his mouth go dry when he noticed just how wet she was. Placing a knee between her thighs, he hovered over her, kissing her lips first and then working his way down her neck, sternum, and ribcage. Her skin rose with goosebumps as his short beard brushed against her skin.

Positioning himself between her legs, he wrapped both hands around her thighs and pushed them high and wide so she was completely exposed to him before he took a long lick along her pussy. She tasted like heaven, and he was pretty sure as he lowered his mouth to her clit, he was in heaven.

Closing his lips around her sensitive nub, he sucked, making her cry out as her hips jerked against his mouth. He continued to lick and suck until he could feel her getting close.

Lifting a finger to her opening, he slowly nudged his way inside up to the second knuckle before he added a second finger. It was so fucking tight, he knew no matter how prepared he got her, it wasn't going to be comfortable at first. Using his fingers, he slowly moved in and out of her pussy while sucking on her clit at the same time.

"Oh, Daddy!"

Her moans and cries filled the room, and when she started bucking her hips against his fingers, he started thrusting harder until she was screaming out her orgasm.

"Oh, fuck! Oh, my god!"

He licked and finger fucked her through it until he felt her entire body relax and then he started all over again with his mouth and fingers so she'd start building for another orgasm.

The second orgasm crashed through her just as hard as the first and when she reached down and grabbed a fistful of his hair to keep his mouth on her, he nearly exploded in his underwear. His Little girl might not be experienced, but she wasn't afraid to take what she wanted.

Slowly pulling his fingers from her, he stood and yanked down his underwear before getting back on the bed so he was hovering over her entire body. She stared up at him with glassy eyes, and a lazy smile spread across her face.

"I'm going to go as slow as I can, baby, but if you need me to stop, just tell me. My cock is a lot bigger than my fingers."

Biting her bottom lip, she slowly nodded, not seeming to care about his size. "Please fuck me, Daddy. I need to feel you."

Letting out a deep breath, he lined up the head of his cock with her entrance and then lowered his face to her mouth to kiss her. She wrapped her arms around his neck and kissed him back, moaning into his mouth.

Slowly, he edged forward, and as his head nudged into her, she moaned again and then winced as he inched in a little more. He froze, not wanting to hurt her any more than he already had. Pulling his lips off hers, he stared down at her and could see the pain on her face.

"Baby, we don't have to do this."

Her eyes widened. "Don't you dare back out on me now. I want this. It's just gonna take a second."

Nodding, he leaned down and kissed her collarbone, inching in as slowly as he could. It was taking an incredible amount of strength not to come. She was so goddamn tight around him.

It took several minutes before he was seated inside, and he could still see the pain on her face as she chewed on her bottom lip, but when he didn't move, she narrowed her eyes at him.

"Don't stop. Please."

She was going to be the death of him. He didn't know if he would ever be able to tell her no. Pulling out slightly, he thrust back in and then pulled out a little more and thrust back in until her winces turned into moans and she was clawing at his back.

"Daddy! Oh, shit!"

He grinned down at her. "No swearing."

She shot him a look and then threw her head back as he thrust in again. There was no way he was going to last long, but he wanted her to come one more time with him inside her, so he gritted his teeth and fucked her while reaching between them to play with her clit.

Within seconds, she was screaming out for him until he could no longer hold off and his thrusts became wild and frenzied as he chased his own orgasm until it exploded and rocked through his entire body.

Both of them were breathing rapidly as he lowered himself down to his forearms and pressed kisses to her face with his cock still inside. After several minutes once they were both breathing normally, he slowly pulled out of her, making her wince.

"Be right back, baby girl. Don't move."

He got up and went to the bathroom to turn on the bathtub. There was no way she wouldn't be sore for a day or two, but he would make sure to keep her as comfortable and cared for as possible.

Her eyes were closed when he returned to the bedroom, but the lazy smile on her face was still there. Reaching out, he scooped her off the bed and carried her into the bathroom. Thankfully, when they'd designed the apartments, they'd done so with the idea that there might be Littles there so they'd had two-person bathtubs installed, making it so he was able to climb into the bath with her.

He settled her between his thighs and wrapped an arm around her so her back was resting on his chest, and they sat in the steaming water in silence until it started to cool.

Reaching forward, he pulled the drain before standing and helping her up. He stepped out first and wrapped a towel around her, then wrapped one around his waist. Before she could step out, he lifted her and set her on her feet on the bathmat.

"Can we do that again?" she asked as he worked to dry her.

Chuckling softly, he shook his head. "In a couple of days when you're not sore anymore."

She stuck out her lower lip in a pout, so he leaned forward and nipped at it.

"No pouting," he scolded softly.

"But I'm not sore."

Pinning her with a stern look, he cupped her chin. "Because you just soaked in the tub. Give it a bit. We'll see how you feel at bedtime. First, I need to get you fed and then we can relax and watch a princess movie."

She gave him a soft smile as she stared up at him. "You're the best Daddy ever, you know."

"You haven't ever had a Daddy, so how could you know that?"

Shrugging, she grasped his shoulders as he knelt in front of her to pull up a pair of sparkly pink leggings. "I just know. Even though I've never had a Daddy, I've been around Daddies my whole life. All the other guys are good Daddies, but I think you're the best one."

He grinned as he lowered a pink flowy shirt over her head with the word Princess printed on the front. "I think you might be a little partial, but I won't argue with you. I expect a Best Daddy trophy at some point, though."

She burst out giggling and nodded. "Noted."

"Come on. Let's go eat dinner with everyone."

Taking her by the hand, he led her from the apartment, and just as they rounded the corner, he stopped short as Rock walked up to them.

Fuck. This was not how he'd wanted her dad finding out about them, but there wasn't any denying it.

Rock stopped, stared at him, and then looked past him to Remi, studying her from head to toe before moving his gaze back to Kade. Just as Kade was about to start explaining, Rock grinned.

"It's about goddamn time you two figured out you were made for each other. I thought you were just going to stare at each other with hearts in your eyes for the rest of your lives."

Okay, he had not expected that. How the hell was he supposed to respond to that?

"I never had feelings for her until she was an adult," he admitted, wanting to make sure that was clear to his friend.

Shaking his head, Rock slapped Kade on the arm. "I know you didn't, Kade. I know even if you had, you wouldn't have acted on it until she was an adult. You're one of the best men I've ever known, and I wouldn't have wanted Remi to end up with anyone else."

His shoulders dropped as he stared at the older man in disbelief. All this time, he'd been worried about what Rock would think and afraid it would ruin their friendship.

Stepping forward, Kade wrapped his arms around Rock. "Thanks, man."

Rock hugged him back, and when he pulled away, Kade was sure the man's eyes were shining with tears as he pulled Remi into his arms.

"I love you and I'm so proud of you for letting this side of you out. I know Kade will take good care of you."

Remi looked up to her dad with tears dripping down her cheeks. "You knew about me being…"

"Little? Yes, honey. I've known for a long time. I know some of it is probably because I wasn't there for you when you were young, and I'm so sorry for that. I wish things had been different."

She swiped at the tears on her face. "It's okay, Dad. I understand. I'm just happy you're here now."

Rock nodded and smiled at both of them before settling his gaze on Kade. "You're one of my closest friends, but if you ever hurt my daughter, I will cut you to pieces and toss all the bits in the ocean. Clear?"

He nodded. "Clear. I won't ever hurt her. She's the piece of my heart that's been missing all this time."

The older man nodded. "I know you wouldn't hurt her, but I just had to make it clear. Now, come on, let's go have dinner."

Remi grabbed both their hands as they made their way into the community room. "I'm going to go ask Bear to make a baked chicken breast and some caulimash for you, Dad."

As soon as she took off into the kitchen, Rock looked at Kade and groaned. "Fuck. I'm never going to get to eat good food again with her hanging around here more."

Kade laughed. "Guess you better find your own Little to fuss over you so she doesn't worry so much."

Rock grunted and shook his head. "I don't think so. But never say never, I guess. I'm going to go grab fries from the table before she comes back out. Excuse me."

Chuckling, Kade nodded and went into the kitchen where Remi was giving Bear strict instructions for no oil or butter to be used on her dad's dinner.

Kade walked up behind her and wrapped his arms around her. "Your dad is a big boy and can make his own choices for food, Princess."

She turned and narrowed her eyes at him, putting her hands on her hips. "Unless you want dry chicken and cauli-mash, I suggest you stay out of it, Daddy."

Her eyes immediately widened as she realized she'd called him Daddy right in front of Bear, but the large burly man just chuckled.

"It's okay, Remi. You're allowed to be yourself here," Bear told her.

She nodded at him and then turned her narrowed gaze back to Kade, who just put his hands in the air.

"I don't want dry chicken, so I'm shutting up and going to go eat what everyone else is having," he said as he backed out of the kitchen.

As he left, he heard Bear and Remi both laughing and he shook his head. She was definitely going to keep him on his toes, that was for sure. But he wouldn't want it any other way.

Before he made it to the table, Storm and Steele walked up to him with grim looks on their faces and Kade knew something had happened.

"Can we talk in private?" Steele asked.

Nodding, he followed the men down the hall to Storm's apartment. When the door was closed behind them, Steele held out an envelope. "This was left on the gate this morning."

Clenching his jaw, he opened the envelope and pulled out the handwritten letter.

My Little Doll,

Now that I know what you are, I can't wait to make you mine. Your MC boyfriend will be gone soon enough and I'll take his place as your Daddy. It's only a matter of time before you become mine. All mine. See you soon.

"What the fuck!" Kade roared.

Thank goodness the apartments were all soundproofed. He was about to lose his shit, and he didn't want Remi to hear him or for Rock to find out.

"We looked at the surveillance footage of the gate and it was the black truck that pulled up but the guy had on a hood and a face mask so we couldn't see anything," Storm explained.

Kade started pacing. "Who the fuck is this psycho? He knows she's Little and that she's with me, which means he could have been at the bar yesterday."

Steele shrugged. "He could've but he also might have seen you and her coming out of her apartment together. We have no way of knowing."

"We need to take this letter to the police and have them see if there are any fingerprints on it that aren't ours. The other letters didn't have threats but this one definitely does, so we can file a stalking report," Storm explained.

Kade continued to pace for several minutes, raking his fingers through his long hair. Remi would be terrified if he showed her this letter. But how could he keep it from her? He couldn't. She needed to know. Fuck.

"Whoever is sending these letters is dead," he muttered before he left the apartment to go find Remi.

TWENTY-TWO
REMI

Pancakes were quickly becoming her favorite. Especially the pancakes Bear made. He always made them in different animal shapes. And having them for dinner made them even more fun. Gobbling down the last bite on her plate, she turned with a full mouth to look at Kade as he walked into the room, but as soon as she saw him, she knew something was wrong.

Not wanting to alarm her dad, who was grimacing as he took a bite of the chicken he was eating, she stood from her chair and met Kade halfway across the room.

"What's wrong?" she whispered as he wrapped his arm around her to pull her into his chest.

He dipped his head down so his mouth was near her ear. "I need to talk to you in private."

She looked up at him to find him smiling down at her, but she knew Kade well enough to know it was a fake smile.

"Your hands are sticky, Princess. Go to the bathroom and wash them."

Her hands weren't sticky. She'd used a fork and a napkin. He was trying to get her out of the room. Nodding, she looked down at her hands and giggled and then started skipping to their apartment, hoping her dad wouldn't catch on to their terrible acting.

Kade followed her and closed the apartment door behind him, locking it, even though he really didn't need to. No one entered other people's apartments without being invited. It was a club rule.

"What's wrong?" she asked.

When he pulled an envelope out of his pocket, her blood ran cold, and she instantly started shaking as she reached for it. He hesitated briefly before releasing it to her.

As she read the scribbled writing, she felt as though she was going to throw up.

Kade stepped closer to her. "It was on the gate this morning. Surveillance couldn't see who it was."

Her mind reeled. *Doll.* That felt familiar. Someone called her that occasionally, but her mind was spinning so fast, she couldn't remember who or when it was.

"T-they... they're threatening to kill you!" she said, her voice getting higher with each word.

Looking up at Kade, she started crying. He reached for her and pulled her into his arms, but her knees buckled so he scooped her up and carried her to the couch, sitting down with her on his lap.

"No one is going to hurt me, baby. No one is going to hurt you either."

But they could. No one was indestructible. Even Kade. And he was the toughest guy she knew. "I don't understand why they're doing this. I don't even have a clue who it is. I feel like I've heard someone call me doll before, but it could have been some random person at the bar. But this letter, it's sick. It's like they think I'm a possession that they can just take."

She was freaking out. Not only was someone stalking her, but now they were making threats to the person she loved.

Kade stroked her back. "Look at me, Remi. No one is going to hurt either of us. At some point, this person is going to slip up, and we'll find him. We're going to turn this letter in to the police department to search for fingerprints since this fucker is actually making threats this time."

Using the backs of her hands, she wiped at her tears. He reached over to the end table, grabbed a tissue, and started wiping her face before she could stop him. It was embarrassing, but she was too upset to care. She didn't know how he was able to remain so calm when she was freaking the hell out inside. She trusted Kade, though. He would protect her with his life, but if she lost him… she didn't know how she'd survive that. It was crazy how someone could become your everything in such a short amount of time.

"We do know that the person keeps driving the same truck, and there's red paint on the bumper. We have guys riding around town looking for it."

Nodding, she burrowed into his chest and sniffled. "I'm sorry I brought you into all this, Kade."

He shifted, moving her into a sitting position so she was forced to look at him. He slid his hand around the back of her neck and leaned forward until they were forehead to forehead.

"I'm glad you brought me into this. Whoever is doing this is going to pay dearly for scaring my Little girl. I love you, Princess. It's going to be okay. I know it's annoying to have a security detail with you at work but this is exactly why I ordered it. Okay?"

Letting out a sigh, she nodded. "Thank you, Daddy."

"You're welcome, Princess. I'm going to take this out to Steele to turn in to the sheriff and then I think we both need some ice cream while we watch a movie. Yeah?"

A grin spread across her face as she nodded excitedly. "Yes!"

After the movie, she tried to talk her Daddy into having sex again, but when she attempted to straddle his lap and winced, he put a stop to it. Then he carried her into the bedroom and changed her into a frilly nightie that barely covered her bottom before tucking her into bed. The last thing she remembered was him sliding her pacifier between her lips.

She hadn't slept well, though. She'd woken up several times through the night. All she could think about was who could be stalking her. Not wanting to wake Kade, though, she'd stayed still in his arms until she'd drifted off to sleep again.

Now, she was on her way to work being driven by Ink and Breaker, and she was exhausted. Kade had asked her if she needed to stay home, but she'd refused. Staying home would just make it worse because at least if she was at work, her mind would be busy with orders and taking care of customers' needs.

The two men didn't try to chat with her during the ride. She had a feeling they could tell she wasn't in a very good mood. Maybe another round of sex would have helped with that. But her overprotective Daddy hadn't let it happen that morning either. He really didn't follow the "sharing is caring" mantra when it came to his cock. It was sweet that he was more worried about her comfort than his own needs. And based on the erection he'd been sporting in the shower, he had needs for sure.

The day started off as usual. She'd almost always worked the day shift, so she rarely had to deal with rowdy bar-goers late at night. It was typically pretty chill during the day, even though they were consistently busy.

By the time the lunch rush was over, she was feeling her exhaustion. She had a feeling Kade would insist on naptime when she got home. Her concealer could only hide the tiredness so much.

"Hey, doll."

Her blood ran cold as that word sounded in her mind. *Doll. My pretty doll.*

She didn't even have to look to know that voice belonged to Bill. Shooting a look at Ink and Breaker, she forced herself to smile at her customer as she took a step back. "Hey, Bill."

"Get my usual?" he asked.

Nodding, she glanced over at the bikers who had seen the way she'd looked at them and were already moving toward the bar.

Trying to act as normal as possible, she fumbled behind the bar to make his drink as Ink and Breaker came and sat on either side of Bill. The older man looked at the two bikers and nodded. "Afternoon, gentlemen."

Ink gave him a slow nod before looking at Remi. "Everything okay over here, Remi?"

Raising her gaze to Ink, she looked over at Bill and then back at him, hoping he would pick up on her signal.

Her hand trembled as she lifted the glass and set it in front of Bill.

"Thanks, doll," he said as he reached for the glass.

Ink and Breaker were on him before he could even get his hand around the cold drink, pulling him off his barstool toward the door.

Breaker looked back at her, pinning her with the sternest look she'd ever seen on the man's face.

"Call Kade. Do not come out after us," he barked.

Nodding, she ran back to the kitchen where it would be quieter to make the call, only when she got back there, the cooks had their music blasting. Noticing the back door open to the alley, she walked through the kitchen and stepped outside where she could finally hear the other end of the call as Kade picked up.

"What's wrong, baby?"

"The guys, Bill… Bill called me doll… T-the guys took him

out to the p-parking lot... he called me doll," she said as a knot formed in her throat.

Kade let out a string of curse words that were quickly muffled by the sound of several bikes starting up. He was coming, and by the sounds of it, so was the entire MC.

A sound behind her made her spin around but before she could scream, she was silenced by a large hand covering her mouth, causing her to drop her phone as she was grabbed by the other large hand and dragged toward a black truck with red paint on the bumper.

TWENTY-THREE
KADE

"Remi!" he roared.

What the fuck happened? Why had the line gone dead? Steele was riding next to him as they raced through the streets at illegal speeds. Talon, Faust, Storm, Gabriel, Doc, Bear, and several other members of the MC were following them while a dozen men hung back at the compound to keep everything safe and secure there.

"Remi!" he called out again.

No response. Then he heard the sound of squealing tires, making his entire body feel like it was going to explode. Shifting into another gear, he sped up even more. As they pulled into the parking lot of The Hangout, he saw Ink and Breaker holding Bill against the side of the MC van with his hands behind his back. Jumping off his bike, he threw down the kickstand and stomped over to the three men.

"Where's Remi?" he demanded.

Breaker nodded toward the bar. "She's inside."

He started running toward the entrance. "Hold him!"

Before he could even get to the front door, one of the kitchen staff came running out. "Kade, she's gone! Someone grabbed her in the alley."

"What the fuck was she doing in the alley?" he shouted.

The cook looked terrified, but Kade didn't care. The only thing he cared about was finding out where the hell his girl was.

"I don't know. She had her phone, and I guess she stepped out there because of how loud the bar was."

Steele and the rest of the men started cursing as Kade ran around the building to the alley and immediately saw her phone on the ground.

"Fuck!"

"Her tracker. You put them in her shoes, right?" Storm asked.

Oh, thank fuck! He nodded as the men all started pulling up the tracking app on their phones. All the Littles that belonged to someone in the MC had trackers placed in various places, so they always had one on them. Kade had put GPS trackers under the soles of her boots.

"She's still moving. They just turned down Castle Road."

Everyone ran back to their bikes and started the engines without saying anything else.

"Hold him until we say otherwise. Take him to the compound," Steele barked at the prospects who were still holding onto Bill.

The men nodded, with matching looks of regret and anger on their faces.

Placing his phone in the phone mount on his bike, he kept the GPS tracker map on and started racing toward his girl.

It only took a few minutes before they were within a mile of the truck on a two-way highway. Revving his engine, Kade sped up until he saw the tailgate of a black truck with red paint on the bumper. It was driving wildly and as he got closer, he could see movement in the truck.

The driver of the truck must have heard them approaching because they started speeding faster. Not wanting to cause the driver to get into an accident and potentially hurt Remi, Kade kept his distance as he continued to follow them with Steele right beside him.

Kade realized the movement in the cab was Remi hitting the driver. That was his girl. Strong and feisty. And once he got her back in his arms, he would make sure she knew how goddamn proud he was that she fought back. They just needed to stop the truck first without harming his girl.

He pressed the call button on his phone to dial Steele, who picked up immediately.

"What's the plan?" Steele asked.

"She doesn't have her seatbelt on. We can't risk running the truck off the road. Do you still have the spike strip in your saddlebag?"

"Always. Want me to go ahead and lay it down?"

That could work. It would slow the truck down so if they did run it off the road, the crash wouldn't be as dangerous. He just hated the idea of doing anything that could hurt Remi, but they didn't have the luxury of that choice.

"Yeah. Do it. When you get in front of the truck, try to signal her to put her seatbelt on."

Steele nodded. "Got it."

Kade slowed down enough to let Steele get ahead of him so he could get into the cross-traffic lane to pass the truck. The one good thing about the highway they were on was that there was very little traffic on it.

He could see Steele motioning to her as he rode in front of the truck right before he sped up so he could get far enough ahead to have time to drop the strip.

The movement in the cab of the truck stopped, and Kade hoped she'd strapped herself in.

"Strip is down."

Motioning to everyone behind him to slow down, Kade kept full speed ahead. He could ride around the strip, but it would be a disaster if all of them tried, so they had to slow down to give Steele time to yank it back to let them pass.

The truck ran over the strip of spikes and instantly started skidding as the flattened tires squealed in search of traction. Darting around the spikes, Kade continued to follow the truck as it slowed down and then suddenly jerked to the right, going nose-first into the ditch.

Skidding to a stop, he jumped off his bike, letting it fall on its side as he ran to the truck with his pistol drawn. Steele and Storm ran to the driver's side with their guns drawn while Kade went to the passenger side to yank at the door, but it wouldn't budge.

Steele tugged the driver's side door open, and both men dragged the driver out while Kade ran around the truck to get Remi out of that same side. As soon as he was at the door, she lunged at him, sobbing into his chest as he clutched her tightly.

"I got you, baby. My brave girl. Are you hurt?"

She didn't answer him. Instead, she continued to sob, grabbing at his cut for dear life as he pulled her out of the truck. Doc ran up to them with his first aid kit that he carried in his saddlebags, his eyes scanning her body as Kade carried her to the back of the truck. Bear already had the tailgate open so Kade could set her down, but when he tried, she wouldn't let him go.

"Baby, we need to look at you and make sure you're okay."

She finally released him, and when he stepped back to look at her, he started shaking with rage. Her cheek was red and already bruising as though she'd been hit.

Doc took over and started touching her joints, checking for anything broken, but Kade couldn't see anything but red.

Looking for Steele and Storm, he found them standing on either side of the driver where he was face down on the asphalt, his hands zip tied around his back. Stomping over, he grabbed the man by his hair and rolled him over, making him howl in pain.

Staring down at her stalker, he couldn't believe his eyes.

Caspian.

Looking up at Steele and then Storm, the men looked just as angry as he felt. Not able to control his anger, Kade kicked the man in the ribs before he squatted down and grabbed him by his hair again.

"You fucked with the wrong guy," he ground out before punching the man in the face, knocking him out cold.

"Jesus, you didn't have to knock him out. How are we going to explain that to the police when they get here?" Storm asked with an amused expression.

Shrugging, he started walking back toward his girl. "Tell them whatever you want. If I knew it wouldn't traumatize Remi, he'd have a fucking bullet in his head when they got here."

TWENTY-FOUR
REMI

She pushed away the set of hands that were moving over her body as she cried out for her Daddy.

"Remi, it's Doc. Look at me."

Squeezing her eyes closed, she shook her head. "I want Daddy!"

"He's coming, baby, but I need to make sure you don't have any broken bones. Did he hurt you anywhere besides your face?" Doc asked.

She knew Doc. She trusted him. He had been a medic in the military and was the club's honorary doctor, but the only person she wanted was her Daddy. Her entire body shook, and it felt as though each breath burned her lungs more and more.

"Remi, I need you to slow your breathing. You're going to have a panic attack and start hyperventilating. Take a slow breath in. Thatta girl."

Doc's deep voice was smooth like velvet, and it calmed her, making it easier to listen to his instructions to breathe slower.

"Good girl. There you go. Good. Can you open your eyes for me? Bear has a surprise for you."

Slowly, she opened her eyes to find both Doc and Bear

hovering closely. Bear held out a stuffed bear to her and as soon as she clutched it to her chest, she knew everything was going to be okay. Nuzzling her face into the soft fur, she took another deep breath.

"That's such a good girl. Look, here comes your Daddy," Doc crooned.

She looked up to find Kade striding toward her looking absolutely terrified.

"Is she okay? We need to get her to a hospital," he said as he walked up.

It felt as though everyone was moving around her but she couldn't focus on any one thing and everything seemed blurry. Just as Kade reached her, everything started to fade to black as she went limp in his arms.

"Why is she not awake yet?"

"She'll wake up soon. They gave her pain medication, so she's only sleeping. She'll be drowsy for the next several days while she's taking it."

Huh. She knew those voices. Her Daddy and Doc. Why were they talking to each other like she wasn't even there? She was there, but she couldn't see them. Why couldn't she see them? Were her eyes closed? Since she couldn't feel them, she really didn't know. Actually, she couldn't feel anything. Everything felt numb and floaty and kind of funny. What was so funny, though?

"Has the sheriff contacted you to tell you what's happening with Caspian?"

Huh. She knew that voice too. It was Steele's. How many people were there?

"He said to let him know when she's awake and he could come by to ask her some questions for his report, but for now, they're holding him in a cell until they transfer him to a state penitentiary. The sheriff did disclose that Caspian was trying to get revenge for being kicked out of the MC. He knew Remi was a big part of the MC family and I guess he knew I had feelings for her so she was the best target to hurt us," Kade replied.

Caspian. She remembered him. He'd been a prospect for the MC but had been kicked out. Why were they talking about him?

Fuzzy memories flooded her mind. Back alley. Black truck with red paint. Kicking and hitting him as he drove wildly down the highway. The thought of her kicking him so hard he'd screamed made her giggle. He'd deserved it. He'd hit her first.

"She's giggling. Is she dreaming?" Kade asked.

Trying to shake her head, she winced as the pain of moving set in. "Ouchie."

Her throat felt dry and scratchy, and she kind of sounded like a frog when she spoke, which made her giggle again. Everything was so funny.

"Why is she laughing?" Kade demanded.

Doc chuckled. "Because she's high as a kite on pain medication."

"Princess, can you hear me? Daddy's right here."

She could feel him near her, and when she tried to lift her hand to touch him, she was stopped short by some sort of tension pulling her hand the other way.

"Stop moving your hand, baby. You have an IV connected. I'm right here," Kade crooned as his warm hand covered hers.

Letting out a sigh, she relaxed against the bed and faded to sleep again.

It was nighttime when her eyes fluttered open. The lights in the room were dim, and there were big windows off to the side that overlooked part of the city. All the lights down below were pretty. There was a slow beeping noise coming from behind her that was getting on her nerves.

Why was she in a hospital room? And why did she feel so itchy? Looking around as much as she could without moving her throbbing head, her eyes landed on a figure beside her with his head resting on her bed at her knees. A smile pulled at her lips.

"Daddy," she murmured and then started coughing. Her throat was still dry and sandpapery.

Kade immediately sat up and stared at her as if he couldn't believe it was actually her before he rose from his chair and moved up near her head.

"Baby. Oh, God, I'm so sorry," he said, his voice choked up.

Why was he sorry? He saved her. He protected her. She was the one who messed up and walked out into the alley. How stupid was she?

When she tried to speak, she started coughing again. He quickly reached over to a table and grabbed a cup with a straw and held it up to her mouth. It was the best water she'd ever had in her life. Cold and soothing on her throat.

"I'm sorry I messed up, Daddy."

His eyes widened and he shook his head. "What? You didn't mess up at all. I fucked up. I didn't keep you safe."

"I went out into the alley by myself."

"Because you thought the person who was stalking you was apprehended already. It's not your fault, baby. Fuck, I should have had people at the front and the back of the bar. I should have done more."

She started giggling and he looked at her in confusion.

"Why are you laughing, Little girl?"

Reaching out for him, she tugged on the bottom of his cut. "Because we're both blaming ourselves, and it wasn't either of our faults."

He thought about it for a minute before he nodded. "You're right. It's Caspian's fault. But I'm still so upset with myself that I didn't do more to protect you. I feel like I let you down."

Was he crazy? He must have really lost it.

"You didn't let me down. You saved me. You and Steele and the rest of the guys."

Nodding, he leaned down and kissed her forehead. "I'm so glad you're okay. They didn't find anything broken but they did find a lot of bruises and they put you on some pain medication to help with that. Your foot is sprained too."

She grinned. "It was worth it."

He tilted his head and narrowed his eyes. "What was worth it?"

"Kicking the shit out of him as he was driving. The idiot didn't even restrain me other than the child lock on the door and locking the window so I couldn't roll it down. What kind of kidnapper is he? A terrible one, that's what kind."

Suddenly, Kade burst out laughing as he shook his head at the same time. "Oh, my princess. You're so damn amazing. I'm so proud of you for fighting back. So damn proud."

"What happened with Bill?"

Kade shrugged. "Steele called him and apologized for our guys roughing him up and explained the situation. Bill understood and said he didn't have any hard feelings and he was glad we found who was actually stalking you. Bill is a strange guy but after Steele talked to him, we're pretty sure he's harmless."

Oh. Well, that was a good thing. The older man was a bit strange but Remi had never felt any weird feelings from him. He just seemed sad and lonely.

Her eyes felt heavy again. "I love you, Daddy. I'm gonna sleep again."

"Okay, Princess. You sleep. I love you too, and I'll be right here when you wake up."

TWENTY-FIVE
KADE

Waiting for her to wake up again was torture. All he wanted to do was pull her into his arms, take her home, and never let her go again. He was pretty sure his heart would never recover from what had happened, so it wasn't worth taking the risk of letting her out of his sight again.

Doc knocked on the door shortly after the sun came up, and Kade almost hugged the man as he walked in with two cups of coffee in hand. He needed all the caffeine he could get. When she woke up, he wanted to be awake and alert.

"You look like shit," Doc said with a smirk as he handed over one of the hot cups.

Kade smiled. "Now I know how you feel all the time."

The men both chuckled. Giving each other crap was how they bonded. Doc was a good man. Kade hoped he would find a Little of his own soon because he would make a great Daddy.

Heaving a satisfied sigh after swallowing a drink of the steaming bean magic, Kade nodded to his friend. "I owe you one."

Waving his hand in the air as if to dismiss the notion, Doc smiled softly as he looked at Remi. "The nurses said she woke up in the middle of the night. How'd she seem?"

"She seemed good. She was giggling again but it was good to see her laugh. It kills me to see all her bruises. I feel like a horrible boyfriend. I didn't protect her when I said I would."

Doc stared at him for a long moment before he finally spoke. "You saved her, though. Nothing in life is foolproof. Mistakes happen. Learn from it and move on and strive to be the best man and Daddy you can be moving forward."

Raising an eyebrow, Kade lifted one side of his mouth into a half smile. "And here I thought Gabriel was the wise one of the group."

Doc shrugged but his eyes sparkled with amusement. "Where do you think I got that line from?"

"Daddy?"

Both men moved to the side of her bed as her eyes opened. Her gaze found Kade first and stayed on him as she slowly smiled.

"Hi, Princess."

She smacked her lips together, making him remember that her mouth was probably dry from all the medication. Reaching over, he grabbed the small paper cup with a straw in it and held it up to her mouth. A little bit dribbled out of her lips as she drank, and he made a mental note to have one of the guys bring a sippy cup to the hospital if she had to stay another day.

"Thank you," she said shakily.

Setting the cup down, he leaned over and kissed her forehead. "How're you feeling? Do you need some meds?"

Shaking her head slowly, she looked up at him with her wide brown eyes. "Can we go home now?"

"We need to have the doctor come in and examine you while you're awake first, and then it's up to him if he thinks you're okay to go home."

Letting out a loud, dramatic sigh, she stuck her bottom lip out in a pout. "No fair."

Both men chuckled as Kade reached for the call button to alert the nurses she was awake.

"You're gonna think everything's unfair for some time because even if you get released from here, Daddy is putting you on bed rest until I see fit," he told her.

Her mouth dropped open. "Well, that just sucks."

The sheriff showed up at the hospital shortly after she woke up and asked her a bunch of questions. She was finally released to go home around noon, and she could barely keep her eyes open by the time Kade got her back to the compound. Luckily she didn't have a concussion or anything other than a slightly bruised foot and some bruises on her face and body. The doctor had sent home prescription pain medication that would make her drowsy so he'd warned that she'd be a little out of it for a couple of days.

Kade carried her into his apartment, then straight to his bedroom, laying her down on the bed. She was already in a pair of pajamas that Steele and Ivy had dropped off at the hospital before she'd gotten released. Pulling the covers back, he situated her so she was tucked in tightly with her stuffed bear and Binks in her grasp.

There was a light knock on the apartment door so he leaned down and kissed her forehead before leaving the bedroom. When he opened the door, Rock stood on the other side with a not-so-happy look on his face. Fuck.

"Rock."

The older man gave him a sharp nod. "You ever keep

anything from me again regarding my daughter's safety and I'll skin you alive."

"The only reason I kept it from you is because she asked me to, and I'm never going to betray her trust. She didn't want you to stress your heart."

Rock sighed and ran a hand over his face. "She needs to stop worrying about me. I'm a grown man."

Nodding, Kade leaned against the door frame. "I know. But she loves you and wants what's best for you."

"Yeah, well, what's best for me is knowing when my family is in danger."

"I promise if anything like this ever happens again, I'll make her tell you. Deal?"

Rock narrowed his eyes. "It better never happen again now that she's under your protection."

Kade nodded and took a step back into the apartment, motioning for Rock to come in. "It won't. She's sleeping, but if you'd like to sit with her for a bit, you can."

They both made their way into the bedroom where Rock pulled up a chair next to the bed and sat. "You kick his ass for doing this to her?"

Kade chuckled. "*She* kicked his ass. Literally, with her boot."

Shaking his head, Rock smiled. "That's my girl."

"The sheriff stopped by the hospital this morning. Caspian is going to go to prison for a long time. He was already on parole and adding kidnapping, stalking, and assault to that, and they think he'll be in for at least ten years or more because of his criminal history."

Nodding, Rock looked at Kade. "You look like shit. Why don't you go crash on the couch for a while. I'll stay here with her."

He patted the older man's shoulder. "Wake me if she wakes up, please."

"You got it."

"I don't wanna take the medicine."

His Little patient was not a very well-behaved one. She didn't want to take any more medication because she didn't like that it made her so drowsy. She insisted she wasn't hungry every time he tried to feed her and he'd caught her trying to climb out of bed twice.

"Little girl, I'm keeping track of all your naughtiness, and your bottom is going to be really sorry once you're feeling better," he told her with a raised brow.

Her mouth dropped open. "Nuh-uh, you're not keeping track."

Smirking at her, he pulled his phone from his pocket and opened the Notes app before turning the screen to her. He could swear her eyes got bigger and bigger as she read the list he'd already started.

"Now, I would suggest you take your medicine unless you'd like me to add that to the list. Oh, and if you don't take it orally, I'll have Doc come in and give you some medication rectally."

She snatched the tablets out of his hand so fast, he couldn't help but chuckle. Dropping them into her mouth, she grabbed the sippy cup he was holding out for her and drank them down.

"Good girl. I know you don't like being drowsy. I'll call the doctor and see if we can get something that won't make you so sleepy, but you have to keep taking these for now."

"You don't play nice, Daddy."

Grinning, he leaned down and kissed her forehead. "When

it comes to my Little girl's health and safety, you're right, I don't play nice, and I never will."

Her glare softened, and her frown slowly turned up into a soft smile. "I love you, Daddy."

"I love you, too, Princess."

TWENTY-SIX
REMI

> Remi: How are you doing? I haven't heard from you. I miss you. I have so much to tell you.
>
> Carlee: I miss you too! I can't wait to hear it all. I'm good, I started a new job and I've been insanely busy. Let's schedule something soon. Love you too.

Smiling down at her phone, Remi replied and sent a heart emoji. They'd been friends forever and no matter how much time they spent apart, they would always be close.

Sitting in bed for four days straight was getting on her very last nerve. Not only was she feeling antsy, but she was also tired of sleeping. At least the doctor had prescribed her some different medication that would help with her bruises and swelling but didn't make her drowsy.

Kade had brought her all kinds of things to do in bed. Coloring books, dolls, blocks, her sketchpad, a bedazzler toy, plus she'd watched just about every single animated movie Netflix had to offer.

He'd kept her company most of the time, which was good and bad. It was good because she loved spending time with him, but it was bad because she was pretty sure the list of her transgressions in his phone was about a mile long.

Her phone vibrated and when she picked it up, she saw Ivy's name. They had been sending funny videos back and forth to each other over the past few days. Opening the message to read it, a slow smile crossed her face.

> Ivy: Kade and Steele went over to the shop for a bit to look at a bike that just came in. Wanna come play in the playroom?

Without even responding, she threw the covers back and climbed out of bed. Her foot was still slightly tender but she was able to walk on it fine and most of her bruising had faded to yellow. She was actually feeling really good, but for whatever reason, her Daddy wanted her to keep resting. Well, what he didn't know wouldn't kill him.

Tiptoeing out of the apartment, she went straight into the playroom, trying to avoid being seen because if any of the guys saw her, they would for sure tattle. It seemed that all of them were on the same team. Rude. Even her dad was on Kade's side about her staying in bed.

Ivy was already in the room when Remi walked in. Turning, Remi closed the French doors that normally stayed open at all times and then went and sat on the floor next to her friend.

"I missed you!" Ivy squealed, leaning in to hug her.

"I missed you too. Oh, my gosh, you have no idea how

good it feels to be out of bed. Daddy has only let me out to go to the bathroom and to give me a bath and he carries me everywhere."

Ivy giggled. "They are a little over the top, aren't they?"

She nodded, grinning widely. "Yes. But I kind of love that about them."

Ivy handed her a teacup. "How about a tea party? I brought candy and juice."

Nodding, Remi took the cup and together, they had "tea" and "cookies," which were actually grape juice and chocolate. They even included some of the dolls in their tea party, who, of course, didn't eat or drink anything, so the two women drank their share as well.

They were so engrossed in playing and giggling that when they heard the sound of a man clearing his throat, they both squealed and spilled their drinks.

Remi whirled around and looked up at Kade's face, giving him an innocent smile. "Hi, Daddy. I didn't hear you come in. I was feeling better and I was hungry and thirsty so we decided to have tea and snacks."

He took a step forward and she swallowed nervously. Uh oh. He did not look happy. Nope. Not at all. Steele looked just as daunting as Kade but his gaze was fixed on Ivy, who was fidgeting with her hands.

"I'm glad you're feeling better. I guess that means you're feeling good enough to finally pay for all the transgressions you've racked up the past few days."

Crumb.

"But, Daddy, I was hungry."

Raising an eyebrow, he tilted his head. "And what did I say right before I left the apartment?"

Dropping her shoulders, she sighed. "That if I needed anything at all to call you and you'd be right there."

He nodded. "And did you do that?"

She didn't like the direction of this conversation. Somehow, she suspected she was just digging a deeper hole. "Sorry, Daddy."

"Come on. Let's go," he said, reaching down to pick her up.

He settled her on his hip and started walking out of the playroom. Looking back at Ivy, she mouthed "sorry" to her because Remi was pretty sure, based on the look on Steele's face, that Ivy would be getting her bottom spanked too.

As soon as they were in the apartment, Kade sat down on the couch, setting her on his lap so she was facing him. "Getting *out* of bed when you were specifically told to stay *in* bed was very naughty."

"I know, Daddy. I've just been so bored, and I really am feeling so much better. I just wanted to do something other than lay around like a sloth."

She hated disappointing him. Being a brat or intentionally being disobedient wasn't her norm, and it made her feel bad that she'd gotten her friend in trouble. But it was all part of being in this kind of relationship, and while she knew the spanking she was about to get was going to hurt, she also knew she wanted and needed it. She needed a release and she wanted her mind to be clear of all the emotions she'd been holding in the past few days.

"I understand it's boring. But, instead of talking to me about it, you decided to sneak out of bed while I was gone instead of asking me so I could be there with you in case you ended up not feeling well or something."

Well, now she was starting to feel bad. He was so thoughtful and sweet and she hadn't even tried to ask him. She'd just assumed he would have said no. "I'm sorry, Daddy."

Pulling his phone out of the pocket of his cut, he tapped the screen several times. "Not only are we going to address what you did today, but we are going to address you spitting out your medication twice, refusing to eat multiple times, having a tantrum because I made you turn off the TV after watching your tenth movie for the day, sticking your tongue out at me when I told you to take a nap, and bedazzling my cut while I was taking a shower."

Her mouth dropped open. "It's your fault you left your cut on the bed."

Yeah, she realized almost immediately that was not the correct response when his eyebrows pulled together and he narrowed his eyes.

"What were the rules with the bedazzler?"

She sighed and stuck her bottom lip out. "That I could only bedazzle the pictures."

"And is my cut a picture?"

"No."

He nodded. "So you knew it was naughty when you did it."

"Yes," she whispered.

"Anything you'd like to say before we move on to your spanking?"

Raising her gaze to his, she felt her lip tremble. "Do you still love me even though I was naughty?"

His arms tightened around her, and his lips pulled back into a smile. "I love you even more. I'll always love you, Princess. Even when you're naughty. You're my girl and I know Littles misbehave sometimes, and that's perfectly fine. Just know that your beautiful little bottom will pay dearly each time, but I will always love you through it."

Nodding, she snuggled into his chest. "I love you, too, Daddy."

He let her snuggle for a few minutes before pulling her bottoms down, then he gently shifted her until she was over his lap with her upper body resting against the couch.

She hadn't expected him to start the spanking so quickly, making her yelp in surprise. "Ouchie!"

Kade chuckled. "We've hardly even gotten started, Princess."

The noise of his smacks filled the room along with her whimpers and cries as she wiggled across his lap. He paused just briefly to lower his powerful leg over both of hers, trapping her completely in place.

"I don't want you to hurt your foot again by kicking," he murmured before resuming the spanking.

His thoughtfulness touched her. Even while spanking her butt, he was worried about her injured foot. Her lip trembled as tears filled her eyes. How had she gotten so lucky?

As the spanking went on, his spanks became harder and faster until she was wiggling and crying out.

"Daddy, I'm sorry! Ouchie!"

"Is my Little girl going to sneak out of bed again?"

"No, Daddy! I won't!"

Tears dripped down her cheeks as the warmth turned to a sting and then spread through her entire bottom as his hand landed over and over again. Letting out a sob, she buried her face in one of the couch pillows, hugging it close to her chest.

It felt as though his hand covered her entire bottom with each smack, and when he started spanking the sensitive sit spots at the top of her thighs, she started wailing. He stopped as quickly as he'd started and then shifted her so she was sitting on his lap with his arms wrapped tightly around her.

She cried and hiccupped and wiped her nose on the front of his shirt, but the entire time, he continued to hold her and tell her how much he loved her.

"You're my good girl, Remi. I love you so much. I don't want anything to happen to you."

Nodding, she sniffed. "I know, Daddy. But I really am feeling so much better. I'm not really sore anymore and my foot is better and I want to get back to normal life."

He studied her for a long moment before he nodded. "I

want Doc to give you a checkup and give you the all-clear before I give you total freedom. Okay?"

She knew he wouldn't budge on that and at least he was only making her get checked over by Doc instead of having to go to her actual doctor and get poked and prodded. "Okay, Daddy."

"Good girl."

Letting out a sigh, she smiled softly and snuggled back into his chest.

TWENTY-SEVEN
KADE

After sending a text to Doc to see if he could come give Remi an exam, he carried her into the bathroom and set her on the counter. Her face needed to be washed, so he grabbed a washcloth and got it wet with warm water before gently cleaning her up.

"After Doc comes, if he clears you, I want to talk to you about going back to your job," he told her.

She tilted her head. "What do you mean?"

"What I mean is, I found your sketchbook and you're the best artist I've ever seen. I know art is your passion. If you enjoy working in the bar and want to continue doing that, I'll always support you, but if you want to pursue your art and sell your work, I will happily take care of both of us."

He knew it was risky looking through her sketchbook. Especially since several of the pictures she'd drawn were of him before they'd gotten together. She was so damn talented, though, and he had heard her talking to her dad before about trying to sell her artwork. If that's what she wanted to do, he was damn well going to do everything in his power to make that happen.

Nibbling on her lip, she met his gaze. "I've been trying to

sell my art online but because of work and Dad, I haven't had time to really put effort into it to get it to take off. I'd love to be able to make custom art too."

Reaching for her, he cupped her chin. "Then do it. Quit at the bar, baby. Move in with me and let me take care of us while you get going. We could even talk to Atlas and see if he'd be able to help you with setting up a website and all that. He's always been good at that stuff."

Her lips pulled back into a soft smile that had him melting.

"I don't want to put everything on you, though. I'm a grown woman. I should be contributing too."

Raising his eyebrows, he squeezed her chin. "You may be a grown woman, but you're my Little girl, and taking care of you would make me the happiest man alive. Besides, the shop is doing really well so I'm pretty comfortable."

"Really?"

He nodded. "Really. We'll be fine. You might have to cut down on your eyeliner obsession so we don't go broke, but..."

Remi scoffed and playfully smacked him. "I don't have an eyeliner obsession. I like eyeliner a perfectly reasonable amount. I just happen to wear more than some."

Laughing, he wrapped his hand around the back of her neck and stepped between her knees, pulling her head to his chest. "I love you, Princess. Let me take care of us, okay?"

She nodded. "Okay. I guess it could be a good thing. I could make Dad dinner more often so I know he'll be eating healthier meals."

Shit. Poor Rock. Somehow Kade had a feeling he would get blamed for this. "Maybe you should let your dad make those decisions for himself. He's a grown man, baby."

"I know... I just worry about him. I wish he wasn't all alone."

Smiling at his sweet girl, he nodded. "I know, baby."

Dropping her shoulders, she sighed. "Fine. I'll stop making

him healthy meals. I know he gives half of them away to the homeless guy down the road anyway."

Throwing his head back, Kade burst out laughing. "How did you know that?"

Rolling her eyes, she giggled. "Because one day he left the clubhouse right after I dropped off a meal, and I hadn't even pulled out of the parking lot yet because I'd gotten a call, so when I saw him leave, I followed him and watched as he handed the guy the meal."

Oh, boy. His girl was certainly something. He was kind of surprised she didn't make Rock start eating the meals in front of her after that.

Someone knocked on the door, and Kade was pretty sure it was Doc coming to do her checkup. Lifting her off the counter, he set her on her feet and led her to the living room.

When he let Doc in, Remi smiled. "I'm feeling all better."

Doc shot her a look. "Little girls always say they're feeling better because they don't want to have to have a checkup, but we Daddies know better."

She huffed a long, dramatic sigh. "Fiiiiine."

Kade winked at her. "That's my good girl."

TWENTY-EIGHT
REMI

Doc let her sit on the sofa while he looked at her bruises and then examined her foot. He had her stand and walk on it to make sure she wasn't walking with a limp, and then he listened to her organs through his stethoscope.

"She sounds good and the bruising looks like it's healing nicely. I want to take her temperature just to make sure it's not elevated. Sometimes a high temperature is the only symptom of infection, and since she had so much bruising it would be good just to make sure."

Kade nodded. "Definitely. I want to make sure we check every possible thing."

Nodding, Doc stood from the coffee table and faced Kade. "I'll let you undress her and hold her while I do it."

Her eyes widened as she looked at Doc and then at her Daddy. "I don't need to be undressed to have my temperature taken."

Kade walked over to her and sat down beside her. "Yes, you do. Little girls have their temperature taken in their bottoms. Come stand between my legs."

Shaking her head, she tried scooting away from her Daddy.

No way. No. Nope. They were not sticking anything in her butt. Not happening.

"Little girl, you can either come willingly or I can redden your bottom and then hold you down while we do it. It's your choice," Kade said sternly.

She really didn't like either of those options, but she knew he meant it and getting spanked, restrained, *and* her butt probed in front of Doc sounded like a way worse option. She slowly stood and walked to Kade, standing between his thighs.

He looked up at her and smiled. "Good girl. We just want to make sure you're healthy. Besides, getting your temperature taken this way will happen often so you better get used to it."

Well, that just sucked.

Reaching out, he hooked his fingers inside the waistband of her leggings and panties and pulled them down below her hips. "Lay over my lap."

Glancing up at Doc and then at her Daddy, she slowly lowered herself so she was face down over his knees. Doc came over, sat down on the coffee table in front of them, pulled a bottle of lube from his bag, and then revealed the biggest thermometer she'd ever seen.

"Why is it so big? They have the other kind that are little, like just a tiny little tip," she whined.

"Those aren't as accurate as this kind. If you're a good girl, I'll give you some stickers when we're done," Doc promised.

She stuck her lip out in a pout.

Doc handed Kade the bottle of lube. "Do you want to get her bottom hole ready?"

Her cheeks heated and she was pretty sure she was going to die of embarrassment. "Can I have my bear?"

Kade paused. "Of course, baby girl. Doc, can you grab her bear off the bed?"

When he left the room, her Daddy ran his hand over her

bottom. "You're doing great, baby girl. Be a good girl and I'll reward you later."

Oh, she liked the sound of that. Rewards were always a good thing.

Doc came back and handed her the stuffed bear Kade had given her. She squeezed it to her chest and closed her eyes. As horrifying as it was that she was face down over her Daddy's lap with Doc watching, about to get an enormous thermometer stuck up her butt, she was oddly turned on. At least Kade had only pulled her pants down to just under her bottom so her pussy wasn't on display.

She heard the lid pop open and then felt the cold liquid of the lube drizzle into her crack before she felt one of her Daddy's thick fingers dipping between her cheeks to spread it around. He massaged her tight hole for several seconds, which only made her arousal seem to climb higher. When he dipped the tip of his finger into her bottom, she whimpered and buried her face into the bear's fur.

"I think she's ready, Doc."

Doc sat down on the coffee table again. "Why don't you spread her cheeks and I'll insert the thermometer."

Oh, good God. They were going to kill her. She never had a desire to play with two men at once but this whole scene was setting her body on fire.

Kade pulled her cheeks apart, and she knew that forbidden little hole was completely exposed to both of them as Doc slowly pressed the thermometer inside, stretching her just enough for her to squirm.

"Such a good little patient, Remi. I'm proud of you. It will be all over in just a few minutes," Doc murmured.

Her only response was another whimper as Doc twisted the thick thermometer inside her, pressing it in even farther.

When he finally stopped moving it, she turned her head and looked back at Kade. "Is it done yet?"

Using his dry hand, he reached over and brushed her hair

away from her face. "It needs to stay inside your bottom for a few minutes and then it will be all over. Daddy is so proud of you. You're definitely going to get a good-girl reward."

His promise for a good-girl reward was all she needed to hear to make herself relax a little more and close her eyes until she heard a timer go off.

Doc gently pulled the thermometer out of her bottom and brought it up near his face to read it. "Perfect temperature. Go ahead and get her dressed."

Kade lifted her from his lap and had her stand in front of him as he pulled her panties and leggings up. She knew he noticed the wetness between her legs because when she looked at him, he was grinning as he stared at her pussy.

"Good news. You're all cleared to resume your regular activities," Doc said to her before turning toward Kade. "I would give her a bath each night with Epsom salts to help the soreness she might still feel from the bruises, but other than that, you have a perfectly healthy and sweet Little girl."

Nodding, Kade smiled and shook Doc's hand. "Thanks, man."

"Of course. Now, how about some stickers?" Doc asked her.

Bobbing her head up and down, she bounced on her toes as he pulled out a small box filled with all kinds of stickers. It was a hard decision but she eventually found a bat sticker and chose that one.

"Thank you, Doc," she said in a small voice.

He ruffled her hair and waved goodbye to both of them before leaving them alone in the apartment.

Kade reached out and pulled her onto his lap. "Seems like my Little girl liked having her bottom played with."

Heat rose to her cheeks, and she tried to hide her face from him but he cupped her chin so she couldn't.

"It was strange and uncomfortable but also exciting. I've

never fantasized about two men doing something like that to me before. It was kind of hot."

She was embarrassed to admit it, but she also didn't want to keep anything from her Daddy.

His eyebrows furrowed together. "There might be times when Doc and I do stuff like that to you together, but no other man will ever fuck you. You're mine, Princess."

She giggled. "Calm down, Daddy. I wouldn't ever want to have sex with anyone else but you. But that was… interesting… I'm glad he's gone now, though. Can I have my good-girl reward?"

Throwing his head back, he laughed. "Yes, baby. You can have your good-girl reward."

Oh, goody. That made it all worth it.

TWENTY-NINE
KADE

Scooping Remi up off her feet, he carried her into the bedroom and set her down on the bed. Cupping her chin, he leaned down and kissed her. She had been so good for him, he wanted to make her good-girl reward one she'd never forget.

His cock was hard as a rock already and he could hardly wait to plunge into her, but this was primarily about her pleasure.

Lifting his head, he reached for the hem of her shirt and pulled it up and over her head, exposing her creamy soft skin and dark pink nipples. Using his thumb and index finger, he pinched one and then the other, giving it a slight tug. "You're so damn beautiful, Princess."

She looked up at him, her eyes glazed over as he teased her nipples. His cock was pressed up against the zipper of his jeans so hard, it was painful.

He pushed her shoulders back so her upper body lowered onto the bed, then reached into the waistband of her bottoms and pulled them down her legs, leaving her completely naked before him.

"I want to see you," she said quietly.

Smiling down at her, he took off his cut and T-shirt. Her eyes roamed his chest as he kicked off his boots, but when he started unbuckling his belt, her gaze lowered to his hands. When she licked her lips and sat up, her hands coming to the button of his jeans, he grabbed hold of her wrists. "Did Daddy say you could touch?"

The corners of her mouth turned up into a sweet and innocent smile. "Can I touch, Daddy? Please? I want to taste you."

Fuck. She killed him. He had a feeling they could be together for thirty years and he would still react to her the same way when she said those sweet words. "You can touch but you can't taste. I'm already so close to exploding that if you put your mouth on me, we won't make it to me fucking you, and I really want to sink into your tight little pussy."

Releasing her wrists, he stood and waited as patiently as he could while she opened his jeans and tugged them and his boxer briefs down, allowing his cock to spring free. Before he realized it, her mouth was on him, sucking him down so deep, he nearly exploded.

Grabbing hold of her hair, he yanked her head back and narrowed his eyes as he looked down at her. "Naughty girl. I should spank your ass and not let you come for disobeying Daddy."

Her eyes widened. "Nooooo."

Chuckling, he smirked at her. "Then you better be a good Little girl and do what Daddy says. Now, lie back and spread your legs nice and wide."

Her pupils dilated, but she did what he said, and as she spread her legs, he could see just how wet she was. Her pussy glistened, and his mouth practically watered with his need to taste her.

Shuffling completely out of his jeans, he kneeled on the edge of the bed and lowered himself so he was settled between her thighs. Hooking each arm under her legs, he pushed them back high and wide so he could see her pussy and her tight little asshole. He would fuck her there one day. Especially after the reaction she had to the thermometer, but she wasn't ready for that yet.

Taking a long lick from front to back, he grinned as she cried out and her legs trembled in his arms. She was so ready for him and already riding too close to the edge. Lowering his mouth to her clit, he sucked on it as he brought a finger up to her pussy and pushed one inside, curling it so it stroked that special spot inside of her. She screamed out, her fingers clawing at his hair while her entire body shook as her orgasm rocked through her.

Licking up every bit of her cream, Kade groaned. His cock was rock hard for her, but he suspected it might never be soft again whenever she was around. Trailing kisses back up her body, he paused at her breasts to lick and suck her nipples before making his way up to her neck and then her lips, settling his hips between her thighs, lining his cock up to her pussy.

"Look at me, Princess," he growled.

She opened her eyes and stared up at him as he nudged into her, using all of his self-control not to plunge right in. He wanted to watch every little expression that crossed her face as he fucked her.

"Mmmm," she murmured, rolling her head back so her chest lifted toward him.

Lowering his head to her breasts, he sucked and nipped gently on the sensitive buds, but when she wrapped her arms around him and dug her fingernails into his back, his control vanished into thin air and he thrust into her so hard that her head nearly hit the headboard.

"Fuck, Princess. You drive me wild. I have no control when it comes to you."

Biting her bottom lip, she moaned and cried out as he pulled back and thrust in again.

"Please. Harder. Please, please, please," she begged.

Letting out a growl, he did exactly that, he fucked her hard and fast, one hand gripping her hip with bruising force as his other hand was positioned at the top of her head to protect it from the headboard.

"Come all over my cock, Princess. Give it all to me."

She screamed as her pussy clenched down around him like a vise, making his own orgasm explode. As both of them came, they kept their gazes locked on each other, making it feel even more intimate.

When their orgasms subsided and they were left panting, Kade carefully pulled out of her and rolled over onto his back, pulling her with him so she was on top with her face resting on his chest. They stayed like that for a long time until he realized she'd fallen asleep on him. He reached out and grabbed a throw blanket, covering them both before closing his eyes for a nap too.

"You're sure?"

Rock smiled and nodded. "I'm positive. I wouldn't say yes to anyone else."

Wrapping his arms around the older man, Kade slapped him on the back. "I love you. Thank you."

When they released each other and Kade stepped back, he realized Rock had tears in his eyes as he held up a finger for Kade to hold on before the man disappeared into his bedroom and came back a minute later.

"I don't know if you already bought one but if not, I think she'd really love this," he said, holding out a box for Kade.

Looking inside, his breath caught in his throat. Glancing up at Rock, he smiled. "I think she would too. Thank you."

Nodding, Rock stood awkwardly, looking anywhere but at

Kade, and he knew the man probably needed some time alone. Men weren't really good at emotions, and showing emotions to another man was definitely at the bottom of the list of favorite things to do.

"I'll see you later at dinner," Kade told him.

Rock nodded, running a hand over the back of his neck. "Yep. Good luck."

"Thanks, I need it. Hey, can I ask a favor? You have a spare key to Remi's apartment, right?"

When he left Rock's apartment, Kade went to the community room to look for Remi, only to find her in the Littles room sitting on her bottom next to Ivy as they played dolls.

"Hey, Princess. Wanna go for a ride?"

Her eyes lit up and she was on her feet in no time. His baby girl loved riding on the back of his motorcycle almost as much as he loved having her there.

By the time he got her helmet situated and they were on his bike, he was practically shaking with nerves. It was all happening so fast, but he always believed that when you knew, you knew, and he fucking knew.

He took her riding all through town trying to decide where he wanted to take her. There was no plan. He wanted it to be special, but he wasn't a roses and chocolates kind of guy. She wasn't a roses and chocolates kind of girl either. She was an MC princess. His princess. And the MC was as much her home as it was his. Hell, the club was the place he'd first realized he had feelings for her. As she danced and giggled on her twenty-first birthday, wearing a tiara that one of her friends had given her, that's when he just knew, even if neither of them had acted on it for years. She'd been his all along.

Realizing he was searching for a special place that didn't exist for them in the town, he headed back toward the compound. That was their special place. It might not seem romantic to most, but to him, it was meaningful.

When he pulled into the gates, he rode back behind the shop and parked in the space between the two buildings where her birthday party had been held and shut off the engine. She climbed down and pulled her helmet off, running her fingers through her windblown pigtails, a big smile on her face.

"That was fun, Daddy! I love riding with you."

Taking in a deep breath, he set his helmet down on his bike and reached into his pocket before dropping down on one knee. She looked at him with a confused expression at first and then her eyes went wide.

"Daddy, what are you doing?"

"I tried to think of a special place to do this and then I realized the most special place for me is right here because this is where I realized I have feelings for you. This is where I fell in love with you over the past several years and this is where I want to marry you. I love you, Remi. You're my whole world and I want you to be my wife forever. You're it for me. There will never be anyone else in my life. Would you do me the honor of marrying me?"

She brought her hands up to her mouth as she nodded. When he opened the box and she looked at the ring, she burst into tears.

"My mom's ring. You got my mom's ring?" she asked through sobs.

As soon as she stepped close enough, she threw her arms around him and fell into his arms, sobbing loudly as her entire body trembled.

"Your dad thought you might like this better than a new ring, but I'll buy you a new ring if you want."

She shook her head. "No. I want this one. It's so special."

"My hope is that our marriage will be as filled with love as theirs was."

Clinging to him, she nodded. "It will, Daddy. I love you so much. Yes, I want to marry you, forever and ever."

Suddenly people were cheering, and he looked around to find a crowd of people had gathered outside. Smiling proudly, he rose to his feet, pulling Remi up with him and wrapped his arms around her as he pressed a kiss to her lips.

"I love you, Princess."

"I love you, too, Daddy."

"Should we go celebrate with our family?"

She nodded. "We need to call Atlas too. He's probably going to give you the big brother talk, but he'll be so happy. He's always loved you."

Chuckling, Kade nodded. "Okay, baby. We'll call Atlas."

Rock walked up and Remi flew into his arms, hugging her dad tightly. Both of them had tears rolling down their cheeks.

The moment was so special, it made Kade choke up and he had to clear his throat several times before he could speak again. Steele and Ivy came over, grinning. Ivy hugged Remi while Steele slapped Kade on the back and offered him congratulations.

"Let's go celebrate!" Steele announced to the group.

Everyone cheered as Remi came back to Kade and clung to him, a smile stretched across her face.

When everyone headed back inside, she looked up at him. "Can we go to the apartment before we celebrate?"

"Sure, baby. Do you need something from there?"

Her cheeks turned pink as she nodded. "Yes. I need to fuck my fiancé."

Throwing his head back, Kade burst out laughing, but his cock thickened at the thought of it. Smacking her bottom, he led her toward the clubhouse doors.

"I can tell you're going to be a handful, Princess."

Nodding, she giggled. "Yes, but I'm your handful now, Daddy."

"That you are. You have about five seconds to get to the apartment and get naked or I'm taking my belt off and spanking your ass."

She squealed and started running.

"One!"

He could hear her fit of giggles as he took off after her.

"Five!"

"You skipped two, three, and four!" she screamed through her giggles when he caught her and swooped her up into the air.

He carried her into their apartment and nodded. "Yeah, that's because I really wanna spank your ass."

"You just wanna touch my bottom."

"You're damn straight. I wanna touch all of you. You're mine. Forever and ever."

"Forever and ever," she repeated.

"Forever and ever, Princess."

Kade took her into their bedroom and set her on her feet, turning her toward the bed. She gasped as she took it all in.

Every single one of her stuffies was on his bed, arranged perfectly by Ivy before they'd gotten back from their ride.

"My stuffies! How? When?"

Grinning, Kade nudged her forward. "I had a little help but I know you said you needed all of them to sleep."

Remi giggled and climbed onto the bed which was now filled with dozens of stuffies covering most of it and clutched one of them to her chest as she looked up at him with tears in her eyes. "I can't believe you did this. But I've been sleeping so good next to you that maybe instead of having them on the bed, we could display them somehow?"

He chuckled. "Thank fuck because I thought I was going to have to order another bed just so I had somewhere to sleep."

Rolling her eyes, she threw one of the plush toys at him

and laughed when he threw it back at her and then tackled her on the bed, kissing her all over her face and neck until she was begging for mercy.

Rolling onto his back, he pulled her on top of him and cradled her against his chest. "I love you, Princess."

"I love you, too, Daddy. Even more than my stuffies."

And that's how he knew he was the luckiest man in the world and he would spend the rest of his life showing her how treasured she was.

AUTHOR'S NOTE

I hope you're enjoying the Shadowridge Guardians MC series as much as we are enjoying writing them! The next book in the series is Atlas, by Becca Jameson.

Atlas by Becca Jameson

"Baby girl, I'm going to count to three…"

Carlee is doing just fine on her own. She doesn't need a man in her life. They never treat her right anyway. She certainly doesn't need her best friend's brother to swoop into town and take over like he never left her. It takes him less than one day to cause her to lose her car, her job, and her apartment. Now she's furious.

Atlas is in town as a favor to his father to help the MC club. What he's not prepared for is Carlee—a woman he's spent years trying to forget. A woman with cute pigtails, a sassy attitude, a pile of problems, and the need for a good spanking.

She can push him away all she wants, but he won't leave town until she can stand on her own.

Shadowridge Guardians MC
Steele
Kade
Atlas
Doc
Gabriel
Talon
Bear
Faust
Storm

Combining the sizzling talents of bestselling authors Pepper North, Kate Oliver, and Becca Jameson, the Shadowridge Guardians are guaranteed to give you a thrill and leave you dreaming of your own throbbing motorcycle joyride.

Are you daring enough to ride with a club of rough, growly, commanding men? The protective Daddies of the Shadowridge Guardians Motorcycle Club will stop at nothing to ensure the safety and protection of everything that belongs to them: their Littles, their club, and their town. Throw in some sassy, naughty, mischievous women who won't hesitate to serve their fair share of attitude even in the face of looming danger, and this brand new MC Romance series is ready to ignite!

PLEASE LEAVE A REVIEW!

It would mean so much to me if you would take a brief moment to leave a rating and/or a review on this book. It helps other readers find me. Thank you for your support!

-Kate

ALSO BY KATE OLIVER

West Coast Daddies Series

Ally's Christmas Daddy

Haylee's Hero Daddy

Maddie's Daddy Crush

Safe With Daddy

Trusting Her Daddy

Ruby's Forever Daddies

Daddies of the Shadows Series

Knox

Ash

Beau

Wolf

Leo

Maddox

Colt

Hawk

Angel

Tate

Shadowridge Guardians

(A multi-author series)

Kade

Syndicate Kings

Corrupting Cali: Declan's Story

Printed in Great Britain
by Amazon